THE PEAR AFFAIR

THE PEAR AFFAIR

JUDITH EAGLE

illustrated by JO RIOUX

WALKER BOOKS

Text copyright © 2020 by Judith Eagle
Illustrations copyright © 2022 by Jo Rioux

First US edition 2022
First published by Faber & Faber Limited (UK) 2020

Library of Congress Catalog Card Number 2021946760
ISBN 978-1-5362-1703-2

22 23 24 25 26 27 LBM 10 9 8 7 6 5 4 3 2 1

Printed in Melrose Park, IL, USA

This book was typeset in Warnock Pro.
The illustrations were done in pencil and ink and rendered digitally.

Walker Books US
a division of
Candlewick Press
99 Dover Street
Somerville, Massachusetts 02144

www.walkerbooksus.com

A JUNIOR LIBRARY GUILD SELECTION

IN MEMORY OF SELWYN EAGLE,
WHO, JUST LIKE MICHEL, WAS BRILLIANT
AT MAKING WEIRD AND WONDERFUL THINGS
OUT OF OLD STUFF
JE

ONE

You would think, thought Nell as she aimed a kick at one of the marble cats that sat on either side of the front door, *if you named your daughter after your favorite handbag, you would cherish her as much, if not more, than you cherished the bag.*

But Nell's parents did not cherish her. She wasn't sure they even liked her. Today, for instance, they'd actually forgotten about her!

Sometimes Nell stayed at school during vacation time. "Out of sight, out of mind" was one of her parents' favorite sayings. But now the dorms were being fumigated, and all the families had been expressly told that not one pupil was allowed to remain on-site.

Yet even though the Magnificents had received exactly

the same letter as everyone else, when all the other parents started to arrive—surprise, surprise—there was no sign of them. No car swept up the drive for Nell; no mother or father leaped out, calling greetings. And no one, in a flurry of suitcases, hockey sticks, and spinning tires, whisked her away.

Instead, Nell was forced to do what she always did: hang around by the steps, watch as the crowd dwindled, and practice an air of studied nonchalance, as if she didn't give a fig that nobody cared.

"You'll have to make your own way home," the head of school had said, making it sound like a piece of cake and not the epic journey (three trains, two buses, a long walk) that it really was. "I suppose I'll have to loan you the money for the train fare and your lunch," she added reluctantly. "Make sure your parents pay it back."

To make matters worse, the gates to Magnificent Heights were locked when Nell had finally arrived, and she'd had to climb over them, which was truly precarious, and she'd snagged her favorite jeans on one of the spikes.

Nell flumped down on the top step and scowled. She had heard the hateful bag-naming story about a thousand times. The bag had been purchased, Melinda Magnificent liked to recount, during the heady days of her and Gerald's honeymoon, from the swankiest shop in Milan. It was called the Penelope, a chunky affair made of crackly crocodile skin and adorned with a gold chain and diamond clasp. Melinda Magnificent adored that bag. She carried it everywhere and went into paroxysms of rage and despair if there was ever the slightest fear that it might be lost.

"How could I not name the baby," she told her friends, "after my dearest, darling bag?"

Nell knew that her mother did not love her more than her handbag. She knew she didn't love her as much as the bag. She wasn't completely certain her mother loved her at all.

All the Magnificents cared about was expanding Magnificent Foods, their supermarket chain, which already generated gazillions of pounds.

"More stores mean more things sold, more things sold means more money in the bank, and more money in the bank means we can spend, spend, spend," Gerald liked to expound, pound signs practically winking in his eyes. The ping of cash registers was music to the Magnificents' ears.

Nell, however, was a hindrance.

It wasn't unusual for Melinda to mutter that her daughter was nothing more than unwanted baggage. She had used those actual words along with *utter nuisance* and *deadweight*. Nell was used to the comments now, but when she was little, they had pierced her heart like sharp arrows tipped with ice.

"Je t'adore, ma petite," Pear had said when Nell reported what she had heard, tears stinging her eyes. Pear had been Nell's au pair before Nell had been packed off to boarding school. Her real name was Perrine and she was from Paris.

"You're too old for an au pair," Melinda had said on Nell's seventh birthday. "I'm fed up with you two jabbering away in French."

The thought of that day still made Nell burn from head to toe. Pear was the sweetest, kindest person in the whole wide world, more of a parent than Melinda and Gerald had ever been! The day of their parting had been so swift, so sudden, so viciously unexpected, that Nell felt like a wolf had tossed her up in the air and then, with tooth and claw, torn her apart. She still didn't really understand what had happened.

It was a question she had asked her parents again and again. But instead of giving her answers, they had sent her to Summer's End. It was a horrible place, the sort of boarding school where the dormitories are always freezing cold and the food has to be choked down or you will starve.

Nell sighed and stretched her legs out in front of her so

she could examine the damage done to her jeans. With a needle and thread, she could fix them. Pear had taught her to sew. She remembered Pear's hand over hers, the flash of the silver needle, the pull of the thread. Her heart ached a little. She had loved Pear with all her might.

The memories of their time together were far, far away, but they still had a golden tinge: Nell and Pear in the kitchen making banana splits and Pear squirting them with whipped cream mustaches, Nell and Pear playing hide-and-seek or jumping rope with pajama drawstrings, Nell curled up in bed listening to Pear's endless stories about child runaways. The memories were like a glorious patchwork quilt, each square different, pieced together in Nell's mind.

Nowadays, Nell wasn't sure what was worse—being ignored at home or being stuck at school. Then there was the inexplicable fear of the dark, which had struck the day that Pear had left. And the constant feeling of dread that only shifted when one of Pear's letters arrived. For five solid years, Pear had written once a month, pages and pages of loops and swirls, always in turquoise ink. The letters were so rich and so vivid that even if Nell was in the deepest of deep, dark doldrums, they never failed to lift her up. Pear wrote reams and reams about her life in Paris: her tiny top-floor apartment; her cat, Sylvie; her work as an embroiderer for Crown Couture. But best of all was the line that always appeared at the end. *One day I will come and rescue you. Stay patient, my little friend.*

But six months ago, the worst had happened. Pear's last letter had arrived before Christmas.

December 15, 1968.

Nell knew the date by heart because she had read it again and again and again.

After that, the steady flow of letters stopped. January, February, March, April, May, June. Not one letter. Suddenly, there was nothing to look forward to. A cold, sharp stone wedged itself into the pit of Nell's stomach and refused to budge.

Of course *she* had written again and again to Pear's address in Belleville, feverish letters pleading for a reply. Nothing came of it. Nell's feelings had progressed from concern to anger and eventually fear. On very bad days, she was convinced that Pear had abandoned her. On even worse days, she worried that something terrible had happened to Pear.

But what could that be?

Now, after six letter-less months, here she sat between the mean-faced cats, waiting for her parents to remember that they had a daughter. At last, the gates swung open, and the Rolls—was it a new one? Nell was pretty sure it had been red before—purred up the drive.

"Good God, Gerald!" Nell could hear Melinda shrieking before she had even climbed out of the car. She was dressed head to toe in white, as usual, an affectation intended to set off her silvery cap of white-blond hair. "What's Penelope doing here? Is the school year over already? But we're off to Paris tomorrow!"

Nell stood, a tangle of muddy-brown hair, freckles, and torn jeans. Her hand, which she had raised in greeting, froze.

In one fell swoop, the despair that had bogged her down for days and weeks and months disappeared, and a wild thread of hope surged through her.

Escaping to Paris had been something she had planned and hoped and dreamed of for years and years.

TWO

"Don't worry about me, Mummy," Nell heard herself saying, smiling her best, brightest smile. "You can take me to Paris, and you won't even know I'm there. You and Daddy can do all the business things and whatnot that you want, and I'll just look after myself quietly in the hotel." She had followed her parents into the house and stood there, twisting her hair hopefully. At last! Here was her chance to find out why the letters had stopped and what had become of Pear.

Melinda's icy frown melted just a fraction. "Hmmm," she said. "Gerry . . ." She turned to her husband, who was doing some number crunching on the three calculators he carried with him at all times. "Is it too late to get one of those Norland Nanny thingies to look after her here?"

Nell gave an inward shudder. Norland Nannies had been procured before. They dressed in silly uniforms and were so strict you could barely raise an eyebrow without them having a meltdown. *Please, no,* thought Nell, crossing her fingers so tightly that blood couldn't reach the tips, and they started to go a sort of bluey white.

"Probably left it too late for one of those, dearest. They get booked up months in advance." Gerald dragged his attention away from his sums and regarded his daughter. It was the kind of look he reserved for a minor irritant, perhaps, like a particularly persistent, buzzy fly. "You'd better not be any trouble," he said warningly. "We can't have you getting in the way."

"Cross my heart and hope to die," Nell answered, pretending not to notice when Gerald rolled his eyes. "I said I wouldn't bother you, and I won't."

"All right, then," said Gerald reluctantly, tossing the calculators up in the air and juggling them. It was a trick he practiced frequently, not to entertain his daughter, but to impress his suppliers. Catching sight of himself in the hall mirror, he sucked in his stomach and flexed his biceps. Gerald Magnificent was an extremely vain man. "I'll call the travel agency pronto and arrange a room at the Crillon. I doubt there'll be a seat left in first class though."

"No matter," called Melinda, who was already tripping upstairs in her white patent leather boots and trailing a waft of Fleur de Sauvage in her wake. "Penelope likes her independence, and I hate playing Mummy on travel days."

Nell rubbed her nose to ward off a sneeze. "Second class will be lovely, Daddy," she said, and she meant it.

Upstairs, Nell rushed into her bedroom and dragged her escape box out from under the bed. It was full to bursting with pamphlets and maps and newspaper cuttings that she had been collecting for a very long time. Nell was not a spur-of-the-moment person—she was a planner. But here she was, smack-dab in the eye of the perfect storm. The mysterious halt in Pear's correspondence, her own fed up–ness with life in general, and the Magnificents' announcement of their imminent travels meant it was definitely, irrevocably time to act.

She tipped the contents of the box onto the floor.

It had not been difficult to accumulate all this information. Magnificent Heights was located in an area of Kent that bordered the suburbs of South London. It was easy to take a train into Charing Cross and then walk to Voyages SNCF in Piccadilly. Voyages SNCF was the headquarters of the French railroad, and Nell had been making the trip there whenever she was home for school breaks. Anyone could walk in and pick up piles and piles of free leaflets about France. Nell had hundreds of them and had read them all millions of times.

After Voyages SNCF, she'd buy a salami, cheese, and pickle sandwich from the Italian café on Swallow Street and eat it perched on one of the stone lions in Trafalgar Square. After that, she'd make her way to the library on Charing Cross Road. Here she would sit for hours on end reading newspapers and books and magazines. Every so often, she would make notes. Her head and her notebook were full of information about Paris. It was her favorite subject. The sights, the shops, the trains, the food. She had never been there, yet she felt as though she knew it like the back of her hand.

Nell unfolded her favorite map, the one with the streets on one side and the Métro on the other. She had examined it so many times that the creases were almost worn away to holes. A familiar sense of peace stole over her. What a beautiful city Paris was! Pear had told her all about the sweep of the Grands Boulevards, the elegance of the parks, the silver ribbon of the Seine River twisting through the city's heart. Nell had never tired of listening. She always wanted to hear more.

Nell picked up her copy of *The Luxury Hotel Guide*. Hotel de Crillon was on page nine. *The most captivating hotel in the whole of Paris,* the caption read, *a sumptuous historic palace on the Place de la Concorde.*

Uncapping her red pen, Nell returned to the map. Running her finger down the Champs-Élysées until it met the Place de la Concorde, she carefully marked the spot with a red dot. Not far from the red dot was a purple dot: Crown Couture on the Rue du Faubourg Saint-Honoré, the fashion house where Pear worked. On the opposite side of the map, in the east of the city, a green dot marked Pear's apartment.

"You never know when you might need to get from A to B," Pear always said. It was she who had taught Nell how to read maps, and Nell had listened and learned. Now she could recite whole routes, street by street. At least when she got to Paris, she would know her way around.

Nell tucked the map into her suitcase. Next she dug around in her schoolbag until she found the plastic bag full of coins. Pocket money had not been forthcoming from Gerald and Melinda, so Nell had been forced to take monetary matters into her own hands. It wasn't strictly stealing, just quietly taking a few multipacks of Magnificent Candy and selling them at school, a penny apiece. The girls couldn't get enough of them, and it didn't take long for the pennies to become a few pounds. Nell scooped the money into her purse until it bulged. In France, she would go into a bank and change them into francs.

Nell's tummy rumbled, and no wonder—it was eight o'clock! Her last meal had been a dry cheese sandwich on the train. Before that, it had been porridge that was the consistency of glue. And the night before, it had been what the school called hot pot, a layer of greasy potato that covered a mess of gristle and fat.

Nell took the stairs two at a time. Mmm, she could smell chop suey from the Shangri-La. Gerald must have gotten Chinese takeout. But at the dining room door, she saw that every single carton was empty, two sets of chopsticks cast aside. She opened her mouth to complain and then closed it again. Her parents hadn't even noticed her. They were too busy muttering. "It's our best chance," Gerald was saying. "Profits are down. If we don't do something drastic, the board will be onto us. Drat them and their sorry stipulations!"

The board was a collection of gray-suited men in charge of enforcing the Magnificent clause. It wasn't unheard of for them to turn up unannounced, and if it was the school vacation time, they always asked to see Nell.

"Ah, the heir!" they'd say in their gravelly voices, pinching her cheeks while Melinda forced a smile. Then Nell would be dismissed, and the adults would start talking about the "stipulations" again. Nell had no idea what the stipulations were—or the clause—nor did she care.

"It would kill the competition fair and square," said Melinda, "but—"

"Are you eavesdropping?" shouted Gerald, making Nell jump.

"You tiresome sneak!" added Melinda for good measure.

"Sorry," said Nell, swallowing down a protest and twiddling a knot in her hair. She mustn't start a fight, in case it escalated into a full-blown war. She mustn't do anything to rock the boat. Whatever happened, she had to go to Paris tomorrow.

Slinking into the kitchen, Nell got to work constructing a triple-decker sandwich. It wasn't her finest culinary effort: the bread was stale, the cheese was moldy, there wasn't enough ham, and the pickle (it had been the last one in the jar) was suspiciously soft. It didn't matter. Nell knew that most things taste delicious when you are ravenous—especially when eaten in bed.

At ten p.m., after the last crumb had been swallowed and Nell had turned off all the lights except one, she lay there thinking. For as long as she could remember, she had tried to work out what she had done to deserve such horrible parents. It was almost as if they had vinegar instead of blood flowing through their veins. Oh well. She whooshed out a long, anticipatory sigh. At least after tomorrow she wouldn't have to worry about them ever again. As soon as she got to Paris, she'd do them a huge favor and disappear. Then they could have their freedom, and she could have hers.

THREE

It had been a long day. Thank goodness Nell had been relegated to second class. It meant she could read her book in peace and munch on chips to her heart's content, instead of being watched for "manners" in the restaurant car.

They'd taken a train to Dover, then a boat, and then another train to Gare du Nord. Now a taxi deposited them on a corner of the Place de la Concorde. Nell climbed out and uttered a small gasp. It was as if she'd stepped into one of those 3D postcards, the ones that shimmer and shine when you turn them this way and that. Maybe it was because it was dusk and the streetlamps were just coming on, twinkling in the mauve-blue light; maybe it was the exhilaration rushing through her because she was finally here. Whatever it was, it felt like magic hung in the air.

Behind her, traffic roared around the Egyptian obelisk, a needle pricking the darkening sky. Ahead, the hotel rose up like a palace, just as it had been described in *The Luxury Hotel Guide.*

"Stop gawking, Penelope, and come on," said Gerald, ignoring the pile of luggage at his feet and starting up the steps.

"Shouldn't we . . . ?" began Nell. Surely they weren't just going to leave their luggage scattered on the sidewalk? Was that normal at a posh hotel? But as usual, her parents were not listening to her. They had already disappeared through the swinging doors.

"Fais attention, petite bourgeoise." Someone was tugging her suitcase from her hands.

It was a boy, about her age, dressed in a scarlet uniform trimmed with shiny gilt buttons and a matching cap perched on his head. He looked as though he'd stepped straight out of an old-fashioned storybook. In a flash, he had grabbed Gerald's suitcase in one hand, Melinda's in the other, and balanced Nell's on his head before dashing up the steps.

The words had been uttered in French. But Nell had understood them all right. "Watch it, rich girl." He had meant to insult her, and he had.

"What did he say?" Melinda asked as Nell pushed through the doors. Despite her lack of interest in her daughter, Melinda always wanted to know exactly what was going on, even if it had nothing to do with her.

The boy, by the entrance to the elevators, was busily piling the suitcases onto a cart. Hearing Melinda's words, he looked up and locked eyes with Nell, as if bracing himself for her complaint.

"Nothing, Mummy," said Nell. She wasn't going to give him the satisfaction of thinking she was a tattletale or that she had understood his insult perfectly well. All the same, she shot him her best scathing look.

While Melinda and Gerald checked in, Nell fumed. She wasn't a rich girl! Was she? She looked down and cringed. She was wearing one of the horrid dresses Melinda insisted upon, made of stiff purple satin with a silly sash thing that stuck out at the side. And it's true that her parents were extraordinarily wealthy. The girls at school thought they were the height of glamour. They often commented on Melinda's glacial beauty and then stared wonderingly at Nell's tangled brown hair and freckles, not needing to say anything because their expressions said it all.

Nell didn't feel rich. For a start, she had never stayed in a hotel as grand as this before! She wanted to tell the boy that, make him see. Explain that her parents never took her anywhere, that they preferred to leave her behind.

But by the time they had checked in and her parents had disappeared into their suite and told her to order room service because they were going out for dinner, she was more relieved than sorry to find that the bellboy had already deposited her suitcase in her room and disappeared.

Anyway, she had the room to admire. The view from the window was stupendous—she could see all the way to the Eiffel Tower—and the room itself was four times the size of her bedroom at Magnificent Heights. The bed was strewn with satin cushions, and the mattress was so springy and plump it made her feel like she was in *The Princess and the Pea*. Everything was delightful: the dusky-pink floor-to-ceiling curtains made from a plush velvet, the soft cream carpet scattered with pretty rosebuds, the walnut dressing table that had been polished to a gleam.

Nell flung off the hateful dress, leaving it in a crumple on the floor, and quickly changed into her jeans and sweatshirt. Then, flicking on the television, she bounced onto the bed.

"Another boulangerie has closed, this time in the tenth arrondissement," intoned a newsreader with an air of solemnity. She was speaking French, and Nell realized with a thrill that she could understand every word. "This adds to the scores that have already shut their doors in the last few months. Investigators are currently exploring the mysterious spore—nicknamed the Thing by Parisians—that appears to be contaminating both the premises and the bread. The question everyone's asking is: Where will they go to buy their baguettes if the Thing continues to spread?"

Nell got up and turned off the television. Outside, the sky had changed to indigo. It would soon be dark: reason enough to stay in tonight and find Pear tomorrow. A card on the bedside table told her to dial one-zero-zero to order room service, so she picked up the fancy gold telephone and ordered Pear's favorite, a croque monsieur and a *chocolat chaud*.

Flinging herself back, she closed her eyes and conjured up her patchwork of Pear. Here was Pear, head bent, needle flashing, stitching pictures of animals onto Nell's bedspread; here they both were, Pear and Nell, heads thrown back, singing "The Flower Duet." After Pear had left, Nell had tried to sing it on her own, but it wasn't the same. Gerald had told her to shut up—said it sounded like caterwauling. He was always so rude.

Nell had just moved on to one of her favorite squares,

a picture of her and Pear eating raclette—boiled potatoes smothered in melted cheese and served with knobbly pickles—when an almighty crash jolted her out of her reverie. Sliding off the bed, she rushed over to the door and peered into the corridor. It was the bellboy, kneeling with his back to her and scrabbling to retrieve a domed silver lid that had rolled under his cart. His cap had slipped to reveal a startling shock of golden-tipped, blazing-orange hair.

"Fais attention, garçon," she said.

The boy jerked around. "You're French?!" he said.

Nell felt a small bud of pleasure unfurl in her chest. Her accent must be even better than she had hoped. "No," she admitted. "Do I sound it? My au pair taught me."

"Well, she did a good job," said the boy. "You sound like one of us!"

Quickly, Nell wriggled under the cart, grabbed the silver lid, and rolled it toward him like it was one of those hoops Edwardian children used to play with. She wanted him to know that she wasn't what he thought she was: stuck-up, or full of airs and graces, or hoity-toity.

"You look different," he said, catching the lid and dropping it back onto the dish with a clink. He followed her into the room, the cart wheels squeaking.

"Probably 'cause I'm not wearing that fright anymore,"

she said, daring a smile and kicking at the crumpled dress on the floor.

"It is a bit of a fright," he agreed, smiling back, a proper smile, like they were equals. Then, lifting the dish high above his head so it balanced precariously on one finger, he sailed past Nell into the room.

"Who taught you that?" she asked in amazement. He was twirling the dish now, so fast that it had gone all blurry at the edges, like a spinning wheel. It was like being in the front row of the circus.

"One of the head waiters," he said proudly, lowering the dish and removing the lid with a flourish. "You should have seen him! He could spin six dinner plates at the same time!"

"Oh! I'd love to see that," she said.

"Not likely. He's miles away, at the Negresco in Nice. The fanciest hotel on the Promenade des Anglais. It's got a pink roof. Looks like a strawberry ice cream."

Nell had seen pictures of Nice in the brochures she had collected from Voyages SNCF. The French Riviera was a glamorous place full of sports cars and film stars, with a circle of palm trees surrounding the bay and the sun shining all day long.

"Do you live here?" she asked the boy.

"Yeah, with my granddad," he said. "He got me this job

just for the summer. Said it would keep me out of trouble. And look! It pays well, too." He dug his hand deep in his pocket and drew out a handful of shiny francs. "I've already earned enough tips today to buy a great big *chocolat Liégeois*."

Nell wasn't sure what a *chocolat Liégeois* was, but it must have been pretty special because just the mention of it was making the boy's eyes sparkle. He seemed nice. His name was Xavier and he was twelve, just like her. Quite suddenly, she realized she didn't want him to go.

"Can I try?"

"Of course you can, you ordered it!"

"Not that!" She laughed. He thought she meant the toasted cheese-and-ham sandwich. "Twirling the plate! You make it look so easy!"

"But it takes hours of practice!" said the boy. "And I've got to deliver raspberry jelly to Madame Tristesse in room fifty-nine—if I'm late, she won't be happy . . ."

"Oh, I'm sure she wouldn't mind waiting just this once. Please . . ." Nell pleaded.

The boy hesitated, and then all in a rush he relented; setting the sandwich and hot chocolate to one side, he showed her how to balance the dish on her index finger. And she managed to do it for about a second before it flew off and nearly crashed through the window. She tried several more times, but at each attempt, the dish clattered to the floor, making them both shriek with laughter.

A thumping sound came from the other side of the wall followed by muffled shouting. *"Tais-toi!"* Xavier's eyes widened and he brought a finger to his lips. "Shh! We're being too noisy," he whispered, but he was grinning. "I'd better go and get that raspberry jelly. Leave the cart in the hall when you're finished and I'll collect it later."

It was very quiet after Xavier left. Nell ate a few bites of croque monsieur and paced around the room, once, twice, like a caged animal. She didn't know why, but she felt a little deflated. She pressed her face up against the cold glass of the window. The lights of the Eiffel Tower winked at her as if it were trying to cheer her up.

She couldn't stay up here! She would explore the hotel. And while she was at it, she'd take the cart back down to the kitchen so Xavier didn't have to do all the work.

The exploring didn't amount to much at first because every floor of the hotel was exactly the same: miles and miles of identically carpeted corridors, cream-colored walls, and blank-faced doors. But when the elevator touched down at the ground floor, Nell sensed a change. Floating across the lobby came the clink of glasses, gusts of laughter, the rhythm of a band. Stepping out of the elevator, she rolled the cart toward the noise.

The room, when she came to it, was heaving, loud and hot, reminding her of the Christmas parties Melinda and Gerald threw at Magnificent Heights. She watched them sometimes from her vantage point at the top of the stairs: tawdry affairs where everyone shouted and no one seemed to like one another very much.

Nell stood on tiptoe peering through the throng. There they were. A flash of platinum hair, a frosty-white satin dress: the Magnificents, deep in conversation with a pouchy-faced, raisin-eyed man. The man raised a hand and clicked his fingers.

Nell watched as a waiter began weaving his way across the room toward them, and then—whoops—the waiter was stumbling, lurching sideways, almost went sprawling, and then—phew!—miraculously, he managed to regain his balance. It was such a brilliant save that Nell wanted to applaud.

But no. It wasn't all right because Melinda was examining her dress, where a tiny splash of champagne had landed, and looking up angrily; Nell's heart sank because she knew that look and then—what?—Nell's hand flew to her mouth. Her chest thumped. Had Pouchy Face just punched the waiter? The waiter was clutching his cheek, his face as white as his jacket. But Pouchy Face had already turned back to her parents and was continuing their conversation as though nothing had happened.

"Get out of the way, will you?" Another waiter squeezed past her with a tray of drinks. "Children aren't allowed in here! It's invitation only. Off you go."

Nell tore her eyes away from the scene, trying to swallow her shock. She couldn't get the picture of Pouchy Face punching the waiter out of her head.

"You tiresome little sneak!"

It was Gerald. He must have seen her from across the room.

"What in hell's teeth are you doing down here? Get back up to your room pronto before your mother sets eyes on you!"

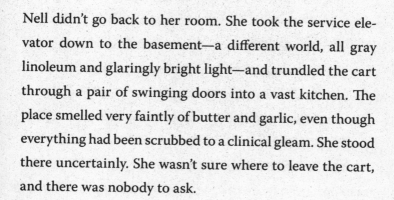

Nell didn't go back to her room. She took the service elevator down to the basement—a different world, all gray linoleum and glaringly bright light—and trundled the cart through a pair of swinging doors into a vast kitchen. The place smelled very faintly of butter and garlic, even though everything had been scrubbed to a clinical gleam. She stood there uncertainly. She wasn't sure where to leave the cart, and there was nobody to ask.

On the other side of the kitchen, a door swung shut. There was someone down here. They'd know. Parking the cart, she crossed the kitchen floor and pushed the door open to find that she was standing at the top of a flight of steps that descended to another corridor. For a moment, Nell hesitated. The stairway was not as brightly lit as the kitchen. What if the light suddenly turned off and she got caught in the dark? But then she heard footsteps ahead of her again, and almost without thinking, down the steps she went, along a brick-walled corridor and through the first open door she came to. The blast of heat was immediate, whooshing out in one great hot rush. She was on the threshold of a room that thrummed with activity. Huge copper pipes crisscrossed the ceiling; banks of dials were ticking and clicking. It smelled of wet dog and hot oil—and was both suffocating and comforting. Everything gurgled and hummed.

Nell stepped inside and then stopped short. On the floor right in front of her was a gaping black hole. And out of the hole stretched a hand.

Nell squished her eyes shut and then opened them again. Was she seeing things?

It was a hand, reaching up from the blackness, searching, grasping, curling, and then it found what it was looking for.

A circular lid lay to one side of the hole, and the hand was gripping it, dragging it, *bump, bump, bump,* across the floor toward the black hole. And then—*clang*—the lid was on.

Nell stared at the spot where the black hole had been.

She knew who that arm belonged to, clad in scarlet with a flash of gilt button at the cuff.

It was the bellboy, Xavier, who only a short while ago had been trying to teach her how to spin plates! And he had actually disappeared underground.

FOUR

ademoiselle?"

Nell whirled around.

An elderly man in blue coveralls was standing in the doorway, regarding her with interest. He carried a newspaper in one hand and a tiny cup in the other. He didn't seem annoyed to find her down there, just puzzled.

"Are you lost?"

Nell looked at the manhole cover, which was now firmly shut, and back at the man.

"I was looking for someone to ask . . ." she said, "about the cart, the cart from room service, and I brought it down to the kitchen, but I didn't know where I should put it, and there was no one there, and then I thought I heard someone." She stopped. She was babbling. If you babbled at the Summer's End School, they gave you six strikes to the hand with a metal ruler. But the man didn't look the least bit angry.

"That was very helpful of you. I'm sure the kitchen staff will be pleased you returned it," he said kindly.

Nell hovered uncertainly, watching as the man crossed the room to a little sink, rinsed his cup, and then filled a small kettle with water. All around them, the pipes rumbled, making a kind of music. The man moved around comfortably, as if he belonged down there.

"I was just going to make some coffee," he said, glancing at her. "Would you like hot chocolate? And a madeleine?"

Nell was hungry, especially since she hadn't eaten all of the croque monsieur. Besides, if she hung around for a bit, Xavier might come back out of the hole. "Yes, please," she said.

The man's name was Michel and he was instantly likeable, not asking too many questions as he fired up a little stove, heating a pot of coffee on one ring and a pan of milk and chocolate on the other. He passed Nell a small oval cake, delicately flavored with vanilla and lemon, and she wolfed it down while looking all around. It was the boiler room, Michel explained, and one of his jobs was to tend the machines and make sure everything ran smoothly. He was also the man who repaired anything in the hotel that needed fixing.

He had made the coziest nook, with the stove, two comfortable chairs, and a bookshelf lined with books and knickknacks. On one shelf was a collection of snow globes, and on another, a string of ancient keys hung like bunting, and here and there, squiggly drawings were propped up between the books.

Nell took down one of the drawings to examine it. It was a very odd picture. On closer inspection, the squiggles looked like a maze or a map of a transportation system, like a more complicated Paris Métro or London Underground.

Michel handed Nell a cup of steaming hot chocolate, and she popped the drawing back on the shelf. He had melted an actual lump of chocolate in it, and she decided she had never tasted anything so good or so very French. If Gerald had been here, his eyes would have exploded with pound signs. It was a million times better than the powdery, watery stuff they sold at Magnificent Foods.

"Do you live down here?" she asked. There was a lovely hominess to the place, what with the murmur of the pipes and all the copper gleaming so comfortingly. But, still, there were no windows. She wasn't sure if she could live without experiencing the pleasure of the sun streaming in or the sound of rain lashing against the glass.

"Almost!" Michel laughed. "Got to make sure everything keeps running—can't have a hotel without hot water and heating, can you? I'm needed at all hours. But no, I have rooms on the top floor of the hotel, so I see the sky sometimes. In any case, I have plenty to do down here. Look at this."

Michel drained his coffee cup and stepped over to a long, low bench cluttered with tools and scraps of metal and wood and other old stuff: candlesticks, cutlery, chipped china. There was a word for it, Nell thought, scrabbling around her brain to find it—was it *detritus*?

"Never throw anything away, that's my advice," Michel was saying. "You can always make something out of nothing. What do you think of this?" Nell looked at what she assumed to be a pile of old junk.

"It's—" she started, and then she saw the expectation in Michel's face and so she looked again, and all of a sudden the pile of junk blossomed into a merry-go-round! It was made from the frame of a bicycle wheel, and hanging from the wheel were spoons and forks and glinting crystal drops that had probably once belonged to a chandelier.

"Go on, turn the handle," said Michel. It was a polished-wood handle of the sort that would once have been attached to a meat grinder. Nell turned it, and the merry-go-round went around and around, and as it did, the crystal pieces winked and the cutlery shone and everything tinkled and clinked together.

"It's beautiful," said Nell.

"Now, it's very late," said Michel. Nell looked at her watch. It was late, almost midnight. She wondered where on earth Xavier had gone. Was he ever going to come back out of that hole? She would have liked to ask Michel about it but decided she'd better not. She didn't want to get the bellboy in trouble. And anyway, Michel was now picking up a little metal toolbox and ushering her out. "I need to do my rounds, and you need to go back upstairs, Mademoiselle Nell, before your parents wonder where you are and call the fire brigade!"

Nell thought that was extremely unlikely and was about to say so, but she was tired. And besides, she thought, as she made her way back—up the stairway, through the vast kitchen, along the corridor, back up in the elevator and into the plushness of her room—the quicker she went to sleep, the quicker tomorrow would come and the quicker she could find Pear!

The next morning, Nell woke to the sound of raised voices. Or rather, one raised voice and some mumbled replies. She lay there for a moment, listening. The argument, if that is what it was, was coming from the corridor, and she was ninety-nine percent sure the raised voice belonged to her mother.

"Penelope!" It was her mother. "Get out here now. I can't make head or tail out of what they're saying."

Nell pushed back her covers and left the warmth of her bed. In the corridor, Melinda, clad in her white satin dressing gown, was clutching a cart littered with breakfast things. The "they" in question were a thin, uniformed man with a long, unhappy face and Xavier, the bellboy. Xavier looked furious, his complexion a deep, dull red.

"He should be fired on the spot," Melinda barked. "Penelope, I need you to translate. Tell him"—she pointed an accusing finger at Xavier—"I saw him, and I know he's a thief!"

Nell felt her whole body go tense. Her mother was always accusing people of things they hadn't done.

"Go on, Penelope!" said Melinda. "Tell him to turn out his pockets!"

Nell stared beseechingly at her mother. "Do I have to?"

Melinda's eyes bulged. "I'm warning you . . ."

"T'as quoi dans ta poche?" Nell mumbled. She wished the floor would swallow her up.

The long-faced man turned to Xavier. Nell could see he was hoping that the boy's pockets were empty.

But Xavier didn't have empty pockets. Sullenly, he withdrew two buns. "What do you care?" he said, low and fierce, in the direction of Melinda but not looking at her. "You'd finished your breakfast."

"What's he saying?" Melinda snapped. "Tell him"—she nodded at the long-faced man—"to dismiss this boy now or I'll call the manager."

"Mummy," said Nell, her mind racing. She had to think quickly. She liked Xavier. He had befriended her yesterday. She didn't want him getting into trouble. "The rolls are for me."

"What?" Melinda's eyes roved over her daughter in disbelief.

"Mummy, listen. I promised I'd keep out of your and Daddy's way today, and I will. I want to go to the zoo, and I asked him"—she nodded at Xavier, who was watching her intently—"to get me some buns so I could feed the elephants." She walked over to Xavier and held out her hand for the buns. "I'm sorry," she said, speaking in French so Melinda couldn't understand, "but she's like this with everyone." To her relief, Xavier gave a tiny nod and Nell nodded back.

"Penelope Magnificent, you stupid, stupid girl," Melinda was saying. "If you want buns for elephants, pick up the phone and call room service! Don't you know anything at all?"

"But I told him leftovers would do," said Nell stubbornly. "The elephants won't mind." She tried a laugh, but no one joined in.

"Oh, for goodness' sake," said Melinda irritably, holding up her hand to stop any further talk. "Brush your hair and go to the zoo. It'll keep you out of the way while we have lunch with the mayor. But be back by five. We're going to Venice tonight. The train leaves Gare de Lyon at eight, and we can't be late."

Venice? It was the first she'd heard of it. They really didn't tell her anything! But it didn't matter. Inside, Nell was doing a wild dance. She had no intention of going to the zoo or of coming back to the hotel afterward! She wasn't going to Venice. By the time Melinda and Gerald got to Gare de Lyon, she would be reunited with Pear!

FIVE

At last, Nell was on her way to Crown Couture, the fashion house where Pear worked. It was the kind of day that can lift your heart no matter *what* your troubles are, bright and blustery with clouds scudding across the piercing-blue sky and leaves blowing skittishly along the sidewalk. Nell skirted her way around the Place de la Concorde and into the Jardin des Tuileries. She could see right away how different these gardens were to the familiar London parks: less wild and altogether more ordered, with avenues of trees marching up and down and ornamental ponds dotted at equal intervals.

Pear was going to get such a surprise when she saw her, Nell thought as she left the park and cut across the

Rue de Rivoli. She patted her bulging bag by her side. She'd packed her maps and a few items of clothing and had her money ready to change at the bank. If Pear wasn't at Crown Couture, she would meet her at her apartment in Belleville. Good riddance to Melinda and Gerald! The thought was even more delicious than the buns she had just eaten. She wiped her mouth on the end of her sleeve, imagining her mother's shudder of disgust. She would never have to listen to her saying "Manners, Penelope!" ever again.

Turning the corner, Nell felt a shiver of excitement.

This was the road she was looking for!

In her letters, Pear had written about the Rue du Faubourg Saint-Honoré. It was the street of the grand ateliers where, behind the elegant facades, in a whirl of tape measure, fabric, and thread, exquisite cloth was snipped, sewn, and—at the hands of the seamstresses—turned into the most beautiful gowns.

Nell could see right away that the road was every bit as luxurious as Pear had described.

Here was the shop selling the finest teas, the elegant emporium displaying the rarest perfumes, and—mmm— Nell couldn't help but pause to admire the confectioner's window showcasing the airiest macarons, piled one on top of the other in clouds of powder pink, pistachio, and the palest blue.

She was here at last. And Crown Couture was just as impressive as all the other establishments on the street, fronted by a huge plate-glass window upon which the trademark crown was emblazoned in gold. Nell pushed through the door and stepped inside.

The first thing she noticed was the smell, which was light and sweet, like face powder mixed with the scent of fresh roses after rain. The second was the music: a waterfall of notes, dipping and rising, a joyous sound that made you think of rivers and lakes and glorious spring days.

The third was altogether more human, clacking angrily across the floor toward her on spiked heels. Before Nell even had the chance to open her mouth, let alone explain, the lady had swiftly placed a manicured hand on her chest and was propelling her firmly backward toward the door and the street.

"Stop!" said Nell, pushing back. The room was entirely white. Melinda would have loved it. White sofas, white flowers—even the clothes on the mannequins were white.

"This is not a place for little girls!" the lady hissed, her French angry and eyes narrowing to slits. "Especially not little girls dressed like . . . street urchins." Her gaze took in Nell's jeans and sweatshirt, and she wrinkled her nose in distaste. "Monsieur Crown will not allow it. You'll give him a heart attack!" She was looking at Nell as if she had just climbed out of a ditch.

"They're clean!" protested Nell, thinking this woman was almost as rude as her mother. "If you don't mind, I would like to see Pear, I mean Perrine Chaumet—she works here."

The woman's beehive quivered. "I have no idea what or who you are talking about. I think you had better leave immediately. And it is not only the cleanliness of your clothes I am objecting to, it is the *look* of them. There is no . . . cut to them at all. You are really spoiling the ambience."

"Perrine Chaumet," Nell burst out. "She's a seamstress, but she embroiders, too. Please show me where she is. Monsieur Crown doesn't have to see me. And if he doesn't see me, he can't be offended!"

"You'll do more than offend him, little girl. It's out of the question." The woman's mouth was set in a determined line, and she motioned impatiently at Nell to leave.

Nell wasn't going to give up that easily, and she was about to say so when a hole suddenly appeared in the wall and another woman, dressed in a white lab coat, stepped out.

"Madame Valérie," the woman said brusquely, looking over her glasses at them with a superior air, "what is going on? We can hear this racket all the way up on the third floor. Is the client here yet? I have six appointments this morning, and you know very well five of them can be difficult."

Nell peered behind the woman. What she had thought was a hole in the wall was actually a concealed door. And behind the door was a flight of stairs.

"Madame Josette—" started Madame Valérie.

But Nell did not wait to hear Madame Valérie's explanation. Pear *must* be upstairs despite what Madame Valérie said, and she was going to find her. Elbowing her way past Madame Josette, she darted through the door and up the winding staircase, ignoring the angry hisses shooting after her. Good. At least they weren't shouting. They must be too frightened to raise their voices in case they alerted Monsieur Crown.

Would he *really* have a heart attack if he saw her? She pictured him setting eyes on her and keeling over, and all because she was wearing jeans! She knew from Pear's letters that Monsieur Crown was an eccentric man, passionate to the point of madness about the creations he designed. But surely he would understand!

Hurrying on up the steps, she reached the second floor and skittered fast past two doors, one emblazoned with M. CROWN, COUTURIER, the other, MADAME JOSETTE, PREMIER. After these was another winding staircase, smaller and more rickety than the first. Up this she went to the third floor. Two more doors. The one on the right read TAILLEUR, and the one on the left read FLOU. Quickly, she pushed open the one closest to her, TAILLEUR.

It was a little, neat room, furnished with about a dozen small sewing tables and the same number of dressmakers' dummies. There were at least twelve women in the room, some sitting at sewing tables, heads bent, intent on the work in front of them; others stood, pins in mouths, tape measures flying, pinning and shaping wools and silks into forms that would soon become dresses and jackets and coats. No one looked up as Nell entered; no one issued a greeting. The only sounds were the snip of scissors, the rustle of fabric, a needle being gently laid down.

Nell searched the rows of bent heads, looking for Pear's curls, coiled like ropes, glinting and golden. Nell remembered how Pear pushed her hair back, tucking the coils behind her ears. Sometimes she wore a ribbon—moss-green velvet or turquoise satin—to hold it in place.

But Nell couldn't see any golden curls or colorful ribbons. The women were dressed in identical white coats and their hair was uniformly unadorned, scraped back tight-as-tight into neat buns and braids.

"Excuse me," Nell said, approaching the young woman sitting closest to her. She was holding a length of midnight-blue fabric, turning and whipping it with deft, invisible stitches. But she must not have heard, because her head remained bent while she continued to sew.

Nell tried again, a little bit louder and clearer this time. "Excuse me, Madame. I am looking for a seamstress called Perrine Chaumet."

At last, the woman stopped and carefully laid her stitching down. Her eyes met Nell's briefly before glancing away. "I'm sorry," she spoke quietly, using the kind of voice teachers at school sometimes called library tones, "but there is no one with that name here."

"But she works here," insisted Nell.

"Hush." A woman working in the next row looked up. "Please be quiet," she said. "Talking is bad for concentration. You heard Claudia. Now, I think you had better leave."

Nell stared at the bent heads. She felt hot and confused. A rush of panic washed over her. Pear had to be here. She had to be! Backing out of the room, she crossed the corridor and opened the other door, the one marked FLOU.

This room looked just the same as the other. Twelve sewing tables, twelve bent heads. But instead of working with plain silks and wools, the fabrics here were sparkling and fluttering with lace and frills and flounces. Again, no one looked up. Again, no one spoke. "Excuse me," Nell began. Everyone ignored her.

Needles flew, scissors snipped, eyes remained cast down. "I'm looking for a seamstress named Perrine Chaumet," Nell said, her voice rising. "Where is she?"

"Not here." An older woman looked up from her work, frowning. "How did you get past Madame Josette? I think you'd better—"

"Go?" said Nell, feeling the anger rise. Why wouldn't anyone take proper notice of her? Why wouldn't they help? "No, I won't go, not until someone explains. I *know* she works here."

"Madame?" A young girl was speaking—very young, Nell thought, perhaps only one or two years older than herself. She had laid down the stuff she was working on and seemed to be appealing to the older woman. A strag-gle of red hair had escaped from the two braids pinned on top of her head.

"Be quiet, Mademoiselle, and carry on with your sew-ing," the older woman spoke sharply. "Your concentration is lapsing again, and you know I promised to inform Monsieur Crown if you aren't up to the work. Think about your mother, now."

"But . . ." The girl turned, and Nell saw a flicker of uncer-tainty in her greeny-gray eyes and understood instantly that the girl knew something and was deliberating whether she should just come out with it and defy the older woman. But as the girl opened her mouth and Nell moved toward her, the door to the studio flew open and a small whirlwind burst in.

"Mon Dieu!" A rotund man dressed in a three-piece, pin-striped suit glared angrily at them. "I might have known it would be you." The man shot an eagle-eyed stare in the direction of the red-haired girl. "No concentration, no con-trol! How do you expect me to create with this cacophony going on? I have five ball gowns to sketch, each to be a tri-umph of form and beauty, and you know very well I cannot do it unless I have utter silence!"

Nell winced. So this must be the famous Monsieur

Crown. She hadn't wanted to get anyone into trouble.

If they would only talk to her, tell her what was going on, then she would leave them alone. The man threw his arms up in the air and brought them down to his head as though in great pain.

"I'm sorry, Monsieur Crown," started the girl.

"Stop!" shouted the little man, holding out his hand. "No more words! Get back to work this instant, and we will review your behavior later." Still quivering, the man turned and came face-to-face with Nell. He stumbled backward as though he had been shot.

"What in the name of God are you?" he said, gasping.

"My name is Nell," she started.

"I didn't ask *who*, I asked *what*!" the man cried shrilly, issuing a fusillade of words that Nell had never heard before. "Madame," he said, appealing to the older woman who had admonished the young girl earlier. "What is it, this . . . *thing*, dressed in denim and a . . . ?" He looked at Nell again, shielding his eyes. "A *sweatshirt*! Blemishing my workroom, sullying my studio. Who let her in? Oh, it's hurting my eyes. Get her out, get her out. I can only have beauty and purity, or all is lost!"

"But I'm looking for Perrine. I know she works here," said Nell in a rush. He had worked himself up into a frenzy. He

wasn't listening to her properly. "Why won't anyone tell me what's going on?"

"Josette, Valérie!" the man shouted, shrill and urgent, taking up a bell like the one they used at school to call them in after break, jangling and jangling it, hurting Nell's ears. "Get her out! Get her out!"

And then Nell's arms were being held, and she was being marched, no, *dragged*, out of the room, along the corridor, down the narrow winding staircase, to the front door, and pushed out onto the street.

"How dare you?" said Valérie.

"This person you are looking for does not work here," said Josette.

"Now, go away," said Valérie, "and don't come back."

SIX

It must be a mistake, Nell told herself as she made her way to the Métro. Pear couldn't have *made up* all those stories about Crown Couture. In her letters, she had described Monsieur Crown perfectly: a pompous, eccentric man who insisted on silence. But there had also been humor in her descriptions, and she had written about the whispering, the stifled giggles shared with the friends she had made in the atelier.

Some friends!

There was only one thing to do. She would go to Belleville, to Pear's apartment, and Pear would be there, with the cat. They would drink tea together and laugh at the misunderstanding; everything would be all right.

In Belleville, the breezy bright-blue day had disappeared. Now the sky was a dirty white, and specks of rain nipped the air. It didn't seem like summer anymore. Nell pulled the sleeves of her sweatshirt down over her knuckles and shivered.

This neighborhood was nothing like the grand Paris she had just left. Gone were the wide boulevards and leafy squares. Here the streets twisted and turned, the higgledy-piggledy buildings jostling together, cramped for space. Nothing was level, with passages and stairways swooping up and down; everything was cobbles and steps.

Nell turned into the quieter Rue Julien Lacroix and then into Passage Julien Lacroix, which veered steeply uphill. She heard them before she saw them, chattering like a flock of sparrows: children, masses of them, crouching at the foot of the steps, poking sticks into a drain, hanging from the railings, racing across the street and back again.

Nell stopped and stared. It was a far cry from the sedate behavior expected of the girls at Summer's End. "Wanna play?" asked a boy who was sitting on the railings, nonchalantly swinging both legs. Suddenly he flipped backward, his legs firmly hooked over the bar, so that he dangled upside down, his green-capped head inches from the ground.

"I'm looking for number seventy-eight," Nell said to his

upside-down head, wondering how the cap was managing to stay on. She would have liked to join in because she'd never swung on bars before. But there wasn't time.

"Use your eyes!" said the boy, grabbing the bars again and unhooking his legs so he became earthbound. His face, flushed from his exertions, contrasted sharply with his grubby hands. He nodded to a narrow door behind Nell, squashed between a boulangerie and a *salon de coiffure*, both shut. Above it, almost faded away, was the ghost of a door number: 78.

"You can try ringing the bell, but no one will answer," said the boy, confidently sauntering over to Nell and adjusting his green cap to a more rakish angle. "They closed it down," he said, indicating the boulangerie, "'cause of the Thing. And the hairdresser's isn't open on Wednesdays. They're the only ones who've got keys." Nell had the impression he was rather enjoying being the bearer of disappointing news.

"Thanks," said Nell, ringing the bell on the shabby door anyway. Just as Green Cap had predicted, no one came. She rang again, her heart dipping down and down.

"Who you looking for, anyway?" asked the boy. A few of the other children had stopped what they were doing and drifted over to see what was going on.

There was no harm in telling him. He might be able to help. "My friend Perrine," said Nell. She stepped back so she could look up at the building. Right at the top was a tiny casement window tucked into the eaves. "That's where she lives." Nell craned her neck for any signs of life, but it was too high up to see. Panic fluttered in her chest. A vision of Pear flashed in front of her, her golden hair spread out on the pillow, pale and listless, unable to move.

"What if she's ill in bed or dying or something, and she can't come down to let me in? I've got to get in there," she appealed to the boy, who was staring at her like she was talking nonsense.

"Have blond hair, did she? Curly? And a black cat?"

"Yes!" cried Nell. "You know her!" Relief flooded every inch of her body, all the way down to her toes. "Knew her," corrected the boy. "Not anymore. She's gone."

"What do you mean, gone? Gone where?" The relief flew away as quickly as it had come.

"Dunno. It was ages ago. D'you wanna see her apartment?"

Nell nodded. All of a sudden, she was at a loss for words.

"We normally use the entrance over the way," said the boy, gesturing vaguely. "But it'll be quicker if we go in around the side. Can you climb?" His look suggested he didn't believe she could.

Nell pointed to the tear in her jeans. " 'Course I can. How d'you think I got that? Climbing over some really tall spiky gates at home, that's how!"

She followed the boy around the corner to an alleyway. It smelled of old cabbage and was crammed with tall garbage cans, one of which the boy clambered on, gesturing at Nell to follow.

"Thing! Thing!" shouted one of the small onlookers. "Watch it, Emil, or you'll catch the dreaded disease!"

"Shut up," Emil said. Standing on tiptoe, he grasped the top of the wall and pulled himself up and over. He made it look easy. Nell's fingers scraped on the rough stone, and her arms ached when she hoisted herself up, but she gritted her teeth, and using every last ounce of strength, she did it, slithering painfully over the top of the wall and dropping down to the other side.

It was a shabby, dirty place, a courtyard enclosed in crumbling walls. Rusty shutters framed dark windows. A line of washing hung damply on one side.

"*Will* we catch the dreaded disease?" Nell asked. She remembered seeing the news on the television last night. Something about a germ contaminating the city's bread supplies.

"Don't listen to that nonsense," said Emil. "My sister told

me the Thing only wants bread, not humans. Look, you can get to the stairway through there." He pointed toward a gloomy-looking entrance. "I'll come with you if you want."

"Thanks," she said, because the hallway looked dark and decrepit, and suddenly she didn't want to be alone. Emil fumbled for a light switch. "It's conked out," he muttered. So they mounted the stairs in the half-light, winding around and around, past the second floor, third floor, fourth floor. In the distance, she could hear a baby crying, the clatter of pans, a shouted exchange. The door to Pear's apartment was right at the top. "Pear?" she called tentatively.

"I told you she's not here anymore," reminded Emil. "But it's not locked. Go in; take a look around."

Holding her breath, Nell pushed the door open and stepped inside. Immediately, she felt a ripple of relief. The apartment was just as Pear had described it: a small, square room, simply furnished. There was the narrow bed with the patchwork quilt, each square a different flower. There were the lemon-colored curtains at the windows, the ones that gently ruffled in the breeze. In the corner was the dresser, and next to it the sink and the age-spotted mirror. A small stove sat in the other corner, and on the folding table next to it, a single bowl. There was something about the bowl, all on its own, that made Nell's heart ache. Slowly, she ran her finger across the top of the bedstead. It was thick with dust. She pulled open one of the dresser drawers: empty except for two tins of cat food.

"Emil, what are you doing?" A young woman was standing in the doorway and looking at them anxiously. At first glance, she appeared to be clutching a furry black scarf thing to her chest, but when the scarf stretched and yawned, and a friendly paw extended, Nell realized it wasn't a scarf at all, but a cat.

"I said I'd show her around," said Emil, indicating Nell with his thumb. "She was asking about that lady who lived here." He turned back to Nell. "This is my sister, Colette."

"Emil!" said Colette. "You know I'm starting my new job today, and you haven't even begun your chores. Sylvie needs feeding . . ."

"Sylvie? Is that Pear's cat?" Nell looked from Emil to Colette. If the cat was here, then Pear must be, too! But Colette was busy shoving the cat into Emil's arms and talking about shopping lists and errands that needed doing, and now she was slinging her bag over her shoulder and backing out of the room.

"Look, I'm sorry," she said to Nell apologetically. "I'm in a tizzy because of this job—what did you say your friend was called?"

"Pear!" said Nell.

"She left ages ago. Asked me to take care of the cat, and I said yes. Emil, wish me luck! Do you really think my shorthand is up to it?"

"Colette's got a job at *Le Monde*, the newspaper!" said Emil with a note of pride in his voice. "She's going to be a famous journalist!"

"I am not!" said Colette. "I'm going to be the editor's secretary. Now, promise you won't forget that shopping, Emil . . ."

Nell's heart lurched. She couldn't let her go. "Please! Where did Pear go? You must know more than that!"

A frown puckered Colette's forehead. "I really don't! Your friend said she'd lost her job and wouldn't be able to pay the rent anymore. It all happened very quickly. Now I must go!"

"How long ago was that?" Nell asked Emil as Colette clattered away down the stairs. She tried to keep her voice level and calm, but inside, her mind was racing. Lost her job? Why hadn't the people at Crown Couture said anything?

"At least six months," said Emil.

Six months! It had been six months since the letters had stopped.

"When will your sister be back?"

"Tonight, I expect," said Emil. "But she doesn't know

any more than she told you. We hardly saw your friend. She worked all hours. The first time Colette spoke to her was about the cat when she was leaving."

Nell moved toward Emil, but he took a step back and held on to Sylvie tight.

"You needn't worry," he said. "I'll take care of her. I'm good with cats."

"Emil!" a faint voice floated up the stairs. "M'sieur's coming."

"Quick, we've gotta go. It's the caretaker," said Emil.

It wasn't until Nell was at the door, turning to take a final glance at the room, that she noticed that one of the patchwork pieces on the quilt had come loose. Or—no—it looked like it hadn't been stitched on in the first place. Crossing back into the room, she plucked it up. It was as light as air, a drift of pale green fluttering in the palm of her hand, exquisitely embroidered with tiny blue birds and pink cherry blossoms.

"Come on. Do you wanna get caught?" shouted Emil from the stairway. Nell stuffed the scrap of fabric into her pocket and ran.

SEVEN

Nell couldn't go back to the hotel. She wouldn't. Pear hadn't been in her apartment for six whole months. She'd lost her job. She couldn't pay the rent. And wherever she'd gone, she hadn't been able to take the cat.

Nell sank down onto the bottom step of Passage Julien Lacroix and thought hard. Someone must know something. Someone must be hiding something. The people at Crown Couture had been weirdly secretive. But why?

The girl, the one with red hair, had been about to blurt something out before Monsieur Crown had arrived. Nell grabbed her bag and began to walk back toward the Métro. The only thing to do was to wait outside Crown Couture for the girl to come out and somehow make her talk.

By the time Nell got back to Crown Couture, it was past three o'clock. Ducking her head so the awful Madame Valérie wouldn't see her, she scanned the hours of business engraved on the door in curly gold script. Closing at six! That was three whole hours to wait! And she was starving. She would go in that café across the street, but first she needed to change her Magnificent Candy money into francs.

Taking a deep breath, she went into the nearest bank, which was a little ways down the street. There were several counters, one of which had a sign above it: BUREAU DE CHANGE.

"I'd like to change this," she said to the lady at the desk, pushing all her coins across the counter.

"You speak excellent French," the lady said with a smile, counting out five francs. It wasn't quite as much as Nell had expected. "Are you on break?"

"Yes," replied Nell, pocketing the money, and then, just in case, added, "my mum's waiting outside."

In the café, she selected a seat on the terrace with a good view of Crown Couture. When the waiter came to take her order, she asked for *saucisse et frites* and a *diabolo menthe* because that was the drink the characters always ordered in her French textbook. The drink when it arrived was luminous green and tasted like toothpaste, and she nearly spat out the first sip. At least that meant she was forced to drink it slowly. There was a long wait ahead.

The hours ticked by. At four o'clock, she ordered a lemonade. At five o'clock, a hot chocolate. Melinda and Gerald would be expecting her now. Would they go to Venice without her? They'd have to. Because she wasn't going anywhere until she'd found Pear. At six o'clock, she ordered a grenadine, and the waiter presented her with the bill. When she saw the amount, Nell tried to hide her surprise. She had just enough money! Out of her whole five francs, she only had thirty centimes left!

At last, the door across the road opened and the *petites mains* tumbled out in twos and threes, stretching and chatting, calling goodbyes to one another. There she was! The red-haired girl. But unlike the others, she wasn't hanging around. Instead, she darted out and rushed off down the street in a flash of blue dress and white tennis shoes.

Nell leaped up, pushing her chair back so quickly that it clattered to the floor. Hastily setting it upright, she grabbed her bag and ran across the street. A car screeched to a halt, a hand on the horn. *"Fais gaffe!"* shouted the driver through the open window.

"Sorry!" shouted Nell.

Oh no! The girl was gone. Or was that her turning the corner? Nell sped up. It was her! She was fishing a book out of her bag now and starting to read as she walked along.

"Please, wait!" shouted Nell. The girl flicked a red braid over one shoulder, oblivious to everything and everyone. She had picked up her pace now, bouncing along in her tennis shoes, her nose still buried in the book. "'Scuse me!" Nell shouted again, louder this time.

Now the girl *had* heard. She stopped. Turned around. Saw Nell. Shut the book and started running.

"No!" yelled Nell. "I only want to talk!" She raced after the girl, down the street, up a wide avenue, zigzagging between pedestrians and trees, into another narrow street, along a passageway, into yet another street. Was the girl slowing down? Nell's heart was pounding, but still she managed to increase her pace. She careened around a corner, and suddenly the girl *was* so close that Nell bashed into her and knocked her to the ground.

"What? How dare you. Get off!" the girl shouted, twisting underneath Nell and jabbing at her with her elbows.

"Not until you tell me about Perrine," panted Nell, clinging to the girl's arm. But the girl wriggled out of Nell's grasp and sprang to her feet. She was strong.

"The woman you are talking about," said the girl fiercely, wrenching away from Nell, who was making a grab for her again, "is a thief! She was sacked! Caught stealing from a client. Is that what you wanted to know?" Furiously, she smoothed the crumpled pages of her book. "Look what you've done!"

Nell stopped, open-mouthed. She hadn't expected this. The fight whooshed out of her body in one fell swoop.

"And also, it's wrong to chase someone when they obviously don't want to be followed. So stop, OK?" the girl snapped. What was she doing now? She was bending down, fumbling for something on the sidewalk. And then Nell's eyes nearly popped out of her head because the girl was actually grasping a manhole cover, her fingers curling around the metal tab, heaving up the lid, pushing it aside, and then clambering down into the blackness below. "I mean it, leave me alone!" the girl said when Nell could only see her head. There was a clang as she reached out and dragged the lid back over the hole. And then she was gone.

That was two days in a row Nell had seen people disappearing underground! She could barely believe what had just happened. The girl had said Pear was a thief. Is that why she had left her apartment in such a hurry? Were the police looking for her? Was she on the run?

Nell bent down and heaved at the metal cover. It made a horrible scraping noise as she dragged it to one side. A gaping black hole stared back at her, taunting her. Despite what the girl had said, Nell knew she *should* follow her. She had a million more questions to ask. The girl must have gotten it wrong.

But she couldn't! Nell's heart was already in her throat just thinking about the blackness beneath her. She felt stupid, helpless. Long, long ago she hadn't been afraid of the dark. Before Pear, she had been fine.

But not after.

Nell stood up and backed away. *Do it, do it,* chanted a mocking voice inside her head. "I can't!" she shouted. Her ears were ringing. She turned and walked blindly back down the street.

"Mademoiselle Penelope!"

Was that someone calling her? She turned around and saw with a flurry of surprise that it was the bellboy Xavier. He was pink in the face, as if he had been running, too.

"What are you doing?" he said. "Your parents sent me to find you. They said you should've been back at five o'clock!"

Hot tears rushed to the back of Nell's eyes. She squeezed them shut to stop them from spilling out.

"Are you all right?" asked Xavier, concern flashing across his face.

"I can't go back," said Nell.

"What do you mean you can't go back? They're waiting for you! You're going to Venice. You'll be able to go on a gondola. See the Bridge of Sighs!"

"I don't want to go on a gondola! Or see the Bridge of Sighs!" exclaimed Nell. "I don't want to go to Venice. I came to Paris to look for someone, but she's disappeared, and . . ." Xavier was looking baffled. It was all too complicated to explain.

"Mademoiselle, please," said Xavier, and now he looked dead serious. "Your mum nearly had me sacked this morning. If I don't return with you right away, she'll get me sacked now!"

Nell was torn. She could refuse to go with him. But if she did, what next? Her plan was in tatters. She had already run out of money. She hadn't even had the courage to follow that girl underground. Besides, Xavier was looking at her with such pleading eyes.

"OK, I'll go back with you," she said. She wasn't sure what else she could do. Maybe she really would have to go to Venice. "But only if you stop calling me Mademoiselle Penelope. I much prefer Nell."

They had barely made it through the hotel entrance when a pale hand clutched at Nell's arm.

"Penelope Magnificent," hissed Melinda, "we have about three minutes max until the taxi arrives. And I WILL NOT travel with you in that state. Whatever will people think?" Her cool gaze swept over her daughter, taking in the torn jeans, the faded red sweatshirt, the messy hair. "Your luggage is over there. Find a dress and get out of those rags."

"And make it pronto," added Gerald. "We haven't got a minute to waste."

Nell's face burned. Everyone in the hotel lobby was staring. Kneeling by her suitcase, she dug out one of Melinda's hateful dresses. It was a horrible salmon-colored thing made from stiff crimplene with a high collar that was itchy and gave her a rash. Thankfully, Xavier had disappeared.

"Over there," Melinda said with venom, nodding to a door marked DAMES.

Nell had only just finished changing and was stuffing her jeans and sweatshirt into her bag when the door banged open. "How long does it take to change into a dress?" Melinda said, tapping her foot impatiently. "I told you to hurry up!"

Nell stared at her, resentment bubbling over, filling

her chest, threatening to explode. She couldn't bear it any longer.

"I went to find Pear," she burst out.

"You . . . what?" Melinda crashed her bag down next to the fancy sinks. A red flush appeared at the base of her neck, blooming angrily up her throat.

"I miss her! I want to see her! I looked for her today. She wrote to me once a month at school, and then the letters stopped. Just like that, *bam!* I know where she works and where she lives, so I thought I'd be able to find her, but I couldn't. She wasn't there." It came out in a jumble, but Melinda's eyes were sharp and Nell knew she understood.

"You promised you wouldn't be any trouble." Melinda was looking at her coldly. "Why didn't I leave you at home?" She turned to the mirror so her back was to Nell, but Nell could still see her in the reflection. Her gaze was stony hard.

"I went to Crown Couture—" said Nell.

"You what?"

"And someone told me she was sacked! For stealing . . ." Nell's voice got higher, louder. The teachers at school would have said she was getting hysterical, but she didn't care. "It's all your fault. Why did you send her away?"

Melinda spun around. "It doesn't surprise me in the least that your . . . friend . . . has been accused of theft. You have no idea what that character is capable of. I told you I wouldn't discuss her with you five years ago, and I'm certainly not going to start now."

There was a knock at the door and then Gerald's voice calling "Taxi's here! Hurry!"

"You heard." Melinda turned back to Nell. "Grab your things and come. And please don't draw attention to yourself on your way out."

The door slammed.

By the sink, crocodile skin and gold glinted under the bright lights.

Her mother had left her be-all and end-all. The bag. Nell plucked it up. The chain clinked against the diamond clasp. Quickly, she pushed open the bathroom door.

On the other side of the lobby, she saw Melinda disappearing through the revolving doors. Gerald would be waiting in the taxi. Any minute now Melinda would realize she'd forgotten her bag. The chain was slippery cold in Nell's hands.

She could walk over there, out of the door, down the steps, into the taxi, and return the bag. Melinda would take it without looking at her. The taxi would pull away. They'd all leave and catch the train to Venice and . . . nothing would change; everything would be the same. She'd never find Pear.

Or . . .

She could run. Get away from them. Set herself free. Out of the lobby she ran, away from the grand hotel entrance, through a door marked PRIVÉ, down a flight of steps, along a corridor, through the swinging doors, and into the kitchen. It was transformed, nothing like the previous night. Now it was a theater of bubbling pots and pans, chopping, stirring, tasting, and everyone far too busy to notice a small girl dressed in salmon pink streaking across the floor and through the door on the other side.

Nell bounded down the stairs and into the boiler room. Slamming the door behind her, she leaned against it, breathing hard. Her heart was hammering, *boom*, *boom*, *boom*, but the room hummed and clicked quietly, warm and cocoon-like, as if it were saying *Don't worry, you're safe now.*

Except she wasn't.

Any minute now Melinda would realize she'd left her handbag in the bathroom. When she found neither Nell nor the bag, she would explode. Every single person in the hotel would be charged with looking for her. Someone would find her and take her back up.

She couldn't bear to go to Venice with them; she couldn't! The thought spiraled up and up in utter panic. A sob escaped her throat. What was she going to do?

Somewhere outside, she heard whistling. Michel. He was just the sort of person to whistle tunes. Would he hide her? Of course not. She hardly knew him. Besides, he was an adult—even if she tried to explain everything, he wouldn't understand.

The whistling was getting closer. Any second now he'd find her. Nell gazed wildly around the room, looking for somewhere to hide.

But already she knew there was only one safe place.

Xavier had disappeared down there the night before. The girl with the red braids had disappeared down one a few streets away just now.

Nell took a step forward and stopped. It would be worse than the blackest nights at Summer's End! Fear clawed at her. She felt clammy and cold. She couldn't do it.

But the whistling was getting closer, and she needed to do something fast. What was worse? Dropping down into the deep, dark unknown? Or being chained to Melinda and Gerald for the rest of her life?

EIGHT

There was a metal ring in the center of the lid, hinged so it would lie flat. Nell grasped it between her fingers and gave it a big heave. It weighed a ton, too heavy to lift properly, but using every ounce of her strength, she just managed to drag it over to one side. It made a scraping sound and then a thuddy clunk. The whistling was very close now.

Tucking the handbag under her arm, Nell steeled herself. She didn't have to do it. She could stop, go back upstairs, and say sorry, just to keep the peace. But all of a sudden, her body seemed to stop listening to her brain, and she was crouching over the hole and lowering herself down.

For a second her feet dangled, dread fluttered, and she thought she was going to drop into a dark abyss, and who knew what lay below—ogres, perhaps, or slithery underground things—but then her sneaker made contact with something fixed, something stable. A ladder! Slowly, Nell began to descend, her heart in her mouth. Above her, a circle of golden light glowed, warm and welcoming. Below, utter gloom. Nell hesitated again. She stopped as a thought struck her. Xavier had covered his tracks, closed the lid. She climbed back up the ladder, the cold metal chain of the handbag between her teeth. Stretching up, she dragged the lid over the hole.

With enormous relief, she found she *wasn't* swamped in utter blackness. It *was* dark, but a watery light was coming from somewhere below. Down the ladder she went, counting the rungs under her breath to steady her nerves: one, two, three, four, five, six, all the way up to ten. And there, at the foot of the ladder, was the source of light, a plastic flashlight stuck into a jam jar. She picked it up and held it out at arm's length, turning slowly around, full of gratitude for whoever had left it there.

She was standing in an underground cavern, a small oval space with arches at either end. Stretching away from these arches were two tunnels, with flashlights in jam jars at the entrance to both. She traced her fingers down the stone walls, cool to the touch, smooth in some places, jagged and crumbly in others. In the distance, she could hear the drip of water, but otherwise everything was still, quiet.

She didn't feel scared! If anything, she felt strangely calm. The arches, and the soft light, gave the place an almost churchy feel. But which way should she go? Which way had Xavier gone? Had he wedged the flashlights into the jam jars? She was about to take the right-hand tunnel when something made her pause. What was that? Nell stood very still. It was very faint, but she was almost certain it was laughter.

Turning, Nell started to make her way down the opposite tunnel. The passage was dusty and dry, filled with a sort of soft silence, the only sound the crunch of Nell's feet and an occasional murmur overhead—the road, perhaps, or the Métro. Here and there, the ground was littered with small stones, but with flashlights in jars every few yards it was easy to pick a path. The tunnel twisted and turned, smaller passages straggling off from side to side, disappearing into darkness, but Nell kept going straight ahead, the handbag knocking against her hip, the chain getting more and more tangled in the strap of her bag.

Bother! She'd only taken it in a moment of panic. A

tiny act of revenge for all the years of misery Melinda had caused. But she didn't want it. She didn't want anything to do with her mother! Perhaps it would be best if she just dropped it, left it here. But what if someone found it and took it back up to the hotel—then they'd know where she was. Better to hide it. She scanned the wall, searching for a suitable place. Here and there, the surface had crumbled, leaving small hollows perfect for concealing things. Nell shoved the bag into one of the deepest of these recesses. Picking up some stones, she piled them in until the bag could no longer be seen.

She'd barely gone a few more paces when a loud growl, followed by a mad barking noise exploded the silence. Nell stopped. Dogs! Down here? There couldn't be! But the noise didn't stop. Teeth, claws. Grinding jaws. And there wouldn't be anyone down here to control them!

Stay calm. Don't panic, she told herself. *Didn't people always say dogs could smell fear?*

But the barks were getting louder and the noise was deafening, and she *couldn't* stop the fear. Any minute now they'd be upon her, a frenzied pack, scenting her, hunting her, getting ready to maul her.

Nell felt dizzy, the tunnel started to swim, and her ears

began to ring. She wanted to run, but she was frozen to the spot. *Move, move!* she urged herself. With a gigantic effort, she turned and began to stumble back the way she had come.

And then, just as abruptly as it had started, the barking ceased and a voice shouted after her, "STOP!"

NINE

ell whirled around. Someone was standing in the tunnel pointing a flashlight at her, the beam a bright, blinding white.

"Point it farther down, she can't see." It was the same voice that had shouted at her to stop.

The beam was lowered, and out of the gloom a shape took form. Two shapes. Children! All angles and elbows with long wispy hair hanging halfway down their backs.

"Where are they?" asked Nell. It felt like the mad barking was still echoing around her head.

"Who?" said the child closest to her.

"What?" asked the other one.

"The dogs, of course!" said Nell weakly. Her voice sounded thin and wavery. She sat down on her haunches, took some long breaths. The children came closer and stood looking at her with squirrelly eyes. What did they think she meant?

They were twins, she could see that. They were dressed identically, in long shorts and striped T-shirts. For a minute, they stood staring at her. And then they smiled. One jabbed the other in the ribs. Their hands were covering their mouths and they were laughing! Proper laughing, shaking and helpless and clutching their sides. Nell didn't understand. What if the noise of their stupid laughing made the dogs come back?

"See!" said one of them. "I told you it'd work!"

The other one was doubled over, gasping theatrically and gripping her stomach.

"What's so funny?" Nell demanded angrily. The girls at school used to have "in" jokes. If you asked them what they were laughing about, they'd say "Wouldn't you like to know!" and then carry on guffawing hysterically, making you feel even more awkward and left out. These twins were just the same, making fun of her, laughing in long, uncontrollable gasps so that they could barely speak.

"Stop it!" she shouted. "You'll make them come back."

"Did you hear that?" said one.

"Yes," spluttered the other. "She really thinks—"

"I know."

"Think what?" Nell shouted again. She'd gotten her voice back now. She wanted to shake them. They weren't worried about the dogs at all. They were facing each other, grinning, their arms entwined.

"We must stop . . ."

". . . Laughing . . . She's getting mad."

"Sorry . . ."

"When we start, we can't stop . . ."

The twins let go of each other and faced Nell. Their squirrel eyes didn't look mean. They looked a tiny bit apologetic.

"Here, see that?" said one of them, shining a plastic flashlight at something on the tunnel floor. It was the same sort of flashlight that was stuck in the jars that lit the tunnels. Nell moved closer.

"What?" And then she saw what the twins were pointing at. A cassette recorder!

One of the twins knelt down and flicked the switch. The sound of barking dogs filled the tunnel again, ricocheting around the walls, filling Nell's head.

They weren't real!

The other twin flicked the switch off. Silence. They both turned their squirrel eyes back to Nell.

"See?"

"And it worked! It's to scare people off!"

"You were running away!"

Nell felt a rush of fury. It wasn't funny to scare anybody witless! She wanted to take this pair by the shoulders and shake them until they understood. But she was dangerously close to tears, and her legs felt a bit wobbly.

"That was a mean trick to play!" she burst out. "And if you didn't want me to find you, whatever it is you're doing down here, why did you even bother to stop me when I was about to run away?"

"Xavier said we should see who it was—"

"And report back—"

"But you were all on your own—"

"And you looked so frightened—"

"Paulette felt sorry for you—"

"I did not! You did—"

"No, you did!"

"Xavier!" interrupted Nell. "Is he down here now?"

"Yes," said the twin closest to her. "How do you—?"

"We met in the hotel. Can you show me where he is, please?" Nell felt rather peculiar, as though everything solid was melting. Up until two days ago, she had been a planner. Not a spur-of-the-moment person. But now she had actually run away underground with no thought as to what was going to happen next. She needed a plan. She needed someone on her side. Maybe these children and Xavier could help.

"Tell us your name first," said the closest twin.

"Nell," she said. "What about you?"

"Paulette. You can tell us apart by this." The one named Paulette pointed to a freckle, almost black, just above her lip. "He hasn't got one."

"He?" said Nell, staring at the wispy hair tumbling down their backs.

"Yeah, he," said the one without the freckle. "You saying boys aren't allowed to have long hair? Don't you know the Beatles?"

"Yeah, yeah of course," Nell said hurriedly.

"He's Paul," said Paulette. "You can tell it's him because he snorts like a pig when he laughs."

"Do not!"

"Do too!"

Nell followed the twins, lost in her own thoughts as they mock-insulted each other. Xavier had *seemed* friendly. But would he be pleased to see her now? She had done him a favor and gotten him out of a fix that morning. But that fake-dog tape was there for a reason. To keep people like her away.

Her stomach fluttered, as if she were in trouble, being taken to see the headmistress to be caned or something. Nell had been caned once, on the hand, and it had hurt like mad. It had burned for hours afterward and left an angry red stripe across her palm.

"Here we are," said Paulette, standing to one side to let Nell through.

They were at the entrance to a cavern. Nell's mouth dropped open. Whatever she had imagined, it wasn't this.

It was actually lit, with strings of electric light bulbs looped around the walls and strung across the ceiling. A large slab of stone protruded from one wall, its flat top set with tin cups and plates. Surrounding this "table" were several upside-down fruit crates, presumably for sitting. There was a rug on the floor, upon which the twins threw themselves and started to wrestle. There were chalk drawings on the walls and more crates, piled high to make shelves, stuffed with books and games, candle stubs, pencils, and paper.

Nell gazed around, her worries momentarily forgotten. She had never seen a den before, but she had read about them in books and knew she was in one now.

"Mademoiselle—I mean Nell! What are you doing here?" It was Xavier. He was clutching an onion and a knife, and even though he was no longer in his uniform, the shock of his fiery hair made him instantly recognizable.

"I don't want to get you in any trouble," Nell said in a rush, remembering what he had said before about being worried about getting the boot. "But I didn't know what else to do . . ." On the far side of the cavern, on a tiny stove, something sizzled and spat. It smelled rich and savory. Despite everything, Nell's mouth watered.

The twins, who had been practicing backward somersaults, stopped. "We caught her by the tape recorder," said Paulette.

"She was running away!" said Paul.

"You don't have to act so pleased about it!" said Nell indignantly. "It gave me the fright of my life!"

"But that's what it's meant to do," said Xavier. "And anyway, aren't you supposed to be on your way to Venice?"

"I'm not going," said Nell. "I've escaped. And I saw you in the boiler room last night and—"

"You were following me?"

"Yes, no, not really." She remembered how furious the girl with the braids had been. She had warned her not to follow her down the manhole. Perhaps there were rules about who was and wasn't allowed down here. "I just need somewhere to hide."

Xavier set the onion down on the stone table, chopped it smartly into quarters, and then tossed them over his shoulder so they landed with a sizzle in the pan behind him.

"So have they gone to Venice without you?" he said, twirling around and giving the pan a shake. There were five fat sausages in there, too.

"I hope so!" burst out Nell. "I never wanted to go in the first place. I only went back to the hotel because I didn't know what else to do . . ."

"She's a fugitive!" said Paulette, who had wrestled Paul into submission and was holding him prisoner with her elbow and knee. "Come to seek refuge!"

For a minute, Xavier and Nell stood looking at each other. She crossed her fingers, realizing how badly she needed a friend. She was all on her own in Paris with nowhere to stay and no money. She was determined not to leave until she found Pear. But she couldn't do it on her own.

"Well, you've come to the right place," Xavier said, giving the pan a small shake so the sausages jumped up and down. "Sorry about the tape recorder—it's not there to scare the likes of you off."

"S'all right," said Nell. "It's a good invention."

"Is she the one who took the buns? The ones you were

going to give Mimi and Gil?" asked Paul as Xavier slid the sausages onto five metal plates.

"Yes. But I got more from the kitchen. So it doesn't matter," said Xavier. The twins were already gobbling their sausages down, even though they were too hot and they had to take gasps in between bites. Nell stood awkwardly. She imagined biting into one, the juice running down her chin.

"Soutine will be here any minute," Xavier said. "But Neige probably won't be coming. Would you like hers?"

"If you're sure," said Nell, her stomach growling in anticipation.

"Never surer," said Xavier, sliding the last sausage onto a plate, twirling it high above his head and then presenting it to her with a deep bow.

"Thank you," said Nell. She bit into the sausage. It was even better than she had imagined, meaty and juicy, with a warm peppery kick.

"Why've you run away?" asked Paulette.

"Because my parents are idiots," she said.

"Prize idiots," agreed Xavier. " 'Specially your mum."

Nell nodded vigorously. And then, all of a sudden, she was telling them her story, about school and Pear and all her carefully laid plans and the horrible events of today.

It was a relief to let it all spill out and wonderful having a sympathetic audience. She was just getting to the part about Crown Couture when footsteps pounded up the passageway and something that looked like an angel crashed into the cavern.

It wasn't an angel of course; it was a boy, dressed all in white, his chef's hat making a kind of halo, his coat flapping like giant wings.

His expression, however, was far from angelic. He looked crumpled and angry.

"The Municipal Department has blocked my entrance off!" He scowled. "And I had to come the long way around, all the way from—" He stopped as his eyes came to rest on Nell.

"Who's she?"

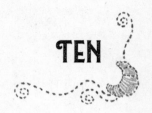

TEN

The boy's name was Soutine and he was training to be a *petit pâtissier*. His parents owned a boulangerie, Chez Ben Amor on the Rue des Martyrs, and all summer, while there was no school, he was learning how to make pastries. He had perfected all the Arabian classics and was now moving on to French favorites.

"Voilà," he said, and with the air of a magician, he produced five squashed mille-feuille out of his bag. The twins groaned appreciatively. "Three layers of puff pastry sandwiched together with two layers of vanilla cream. Papa says to make these takes great skill and daring."

Soutine caught Nell's eye, and his mouth, which had turned up at the corners as he described the cakes, turned down again.

"I haven't got one for you."

"Give her Neige's!" said Paulette. "Xav gave her Neige's sausage, didn't you, Xav? You must be nice, too. Why are you so sulky?"

"It doesn't matter," started Nell. But Paul was laying his pastry down on the table. "It's infected with the Thing!" he said. Paulette giggled and joined in. "Thing, Thing!" they crowed. It was exactly what the children in Belleville had said, thought Nell, a sort of joke, but Soutine reacted furiously.

"It is not!" he said. "I told you *Maman* keeps everything spotless. It's only dirty places that catch the Thing."

"They're joking, Soutine," said Xavier, jabbing Soutine in the ribs. "What's gotten into you?"

"I told you, I'm mad. It's taken me nearly an hour to get here. I had to use the entrance in the crypt at Eglise Notre-Dame-De-Lorette and then there were puddles nearly all the way here, splashing my whites."

As he spoke, Soutine passed Nell a cake and she accepted it, the layers squidging together as she took a bite. The sweet flakiness made it impossible to eat without a smile.

"Do any of you live down here? With no parents?" asked Nell. Perhaps she could hide down here, too. As long as the flashlights were lit, she'd be OK.

"It's not the Victorian times, you know!" scoffed Soutine. "We do all have homes." Nell looked at him, wondering why he was so prickly. He seemed to have taken a dislike to her, and she didn't know why.

"Yes, but in the olden days, people *did* live down here," said Paul. "All sorts: robbers, runaways, even mushroom farmers!"

"There are zillions of miles of passages," said Xavier, springing up, "perfect for hiding in—or getting lost. Look!" He dug about in one of the crates and drew out a handful of squiggle-covered postcards. With a jolt, Nell saw that the squiggles were the same drawings she had seen on display in Michel's boiler room. "Whenever I can, I go exploring and map it all out!" said Xavier proudly.

Nell took the maps and leafed through them. They looked like intricately drawn mazes with teeny-tiny arrows marking out particular routes and minuscule writing that said things like *Puddles* and *Loose chippings* and even one that said *Beware, flooded cavern.*

"These are really good," she said, and she meant it. "It must have taken you ages."

"It's easier than it looks," said Xavier. "Most of the tunnels mirror the streets above. Some of them even have the same road names already scratched into the stone."

"And now"—Soutine kicked the wall, releasing a cloud of dust that made Nell cough—"the mayor wants to take it away from us." He was glaring at her as though it was all her fault. "Why can't he just leave us alone?"

"The mayor?" echoed Nell. Where had she heard that name before? Oh, that was it! After the bun incident, Melinda had said she and Gerald were having lunch with him. She decided to keep this information to herself. Her new friends all appeared to be scowling at the mere mention of his name.

Xavier had left the table and was rummaging through one of the boxes on the shelves. He drew out a newspaper and flicked through the pages until he found what he was looking for.

"Read that and you'll see," said Xavier.

"Aloud," added Paulette, "so we can hear it again."

Nell smoothed the page out. The date at the top read THURSDAY, MAY 29, 1969.

> *"For decades, the tunnels below Paris have been the unchallenged playground of the city's children. This subterranean paradise (once used by French resistance fighters hiding out during the war) dates back five hundred years when*

limestone quarries were first mined to build our great city.

"But since being elected last year, Mayor Monsieur Henri has made it his mission to bring an end to the young people's reign underground. Yesterday, at a conference entitled *Better Lives for Our Children*, he elaborated on his plans.

"'Parents should not be allowing their children to roam below the city,' he said. 'Scientists have expressed concern at the foul air—some would call it a miasma—carrying germs and other harmful properties. From the first of June, the Municipal Department will be closing down all entrances to subterranean Paris. I want our city to be cleaner, brighter, and for our children to flourish in the open air.

"'This doesn't mean playing in the street is a suitable alternative, and we will be clamping down on this habit in the near future. Instead, I will be building municipal playgrounds for our children with fences and gates to keep them secure. Remember, I am doing this solely for the health and wellbeing of our little ones.'"

"What does he know about our health?" exploded Xavier. "I've only ever had chicken pox, and I caught that from my cousin who lives in Bordeaux. I wasn't anywhere *near* Paris or the tunnels."

"I had tonsillitis once," said Paul.

"Oh, don't exaggerate; it was just a sore throat," corrected Paulette.

"What *is* a miasma?" asked Soutine.

"A stink," said Nell, who had learned all about cholera at school, and how people had once thought diseases were caused by poisonous vapors that smelled bad. "No one believes in it anymore. Diseases are spread by germs, not bad air. This mayor of yours should know that." She folded the newspaper and handed it back to Xavier.

"It doesn't smell down here!" said Paul.

"Except of nice things like sausages!" said Paulette. "That's lying, that is!"

Nell sniffed. Now that the aroma of sizzling sausages had dissipated, there *was* a bit of a musty tinge to the air. But it was only an old-cave sort of smell, which you probably got used to after a while. The mayor sounded really mean. The den was lovely. Why would anyone want to close it down?

"That's why Xavier thought of the dogs," said Paulette.

"Scare those Municipal Department men off if they ever dare to come down here."

"Why are you boring her with it all?" huffed Soutine. "She doesn't care. Look, I've got to go. I promised Papa I'd help with the next batch of bread. Will you all come around tomorrow and help break open my entrance again?"

———⌒———

"Is he always so angry?" asked Nell as she followed Xavier up the ladder and back into the boiler room. It was already nine o'clock in the evening, and the others had gone home to second suppers and warm beds. Xavier had said she could tag along with him. He said he knew a place where she could stay. The boiler room welcomed them with a comforting thrum. "Soutine, I mean."

"Just recently," said Xavier. "It's the Thing. He says he's not worried, but he is. He acts like he doesn't care and goes on about his shop being immune because his parents keep it so clean, but he's seen the news like the rest of us. When it strikes, it strikes. Whatever it is, it sets in, and no one's worked out how to get rid of it yet." Nell pictured the boulangerie in Belleville, the one she'd seen earlier in the day, its doors closed, its interior dark. Emil had said that it had shut down because of the Thing. She wondered what would happen to all the bread makers and shopkeepers, the people whose livelihoods had been destroyed just like that, crash bang. No wonder Soutine was anxious.

"Those children you were talking about, Mimi and Gil, the ones you took the buns for . . ." she said.

"The Bernards," said Xavier. "Their boulangerie was closed because of the Thing, and they couldn't pay the rent. They're holed up in a cavern near Montparnasse. Not for long, just until they get themselves sorted. I take Mimi and Gil cakes and buns when I can."

Nell wasn't sure if she had heard right. An actual family underground? "But Paul said people only lived down here in the olden days . . ."

"Yeah, until this Thing started," said Xavier, heaving the cover back over the manhole. It clanged noisily as it slotted into place.

"Xav," Nell whispered, in case anyone else was down there, "I can't afford to stay in the hotel. I've run out of money. And besides, my parents are bound to have come back looking for the bag. I can't let them find me before I find Pear; I can't!"

"I told you I've got an idea, and I do," said Xav. "Look, come this way."

Nell followed Xavier out of the boiler room and farther

along the brick-walled corridor to a room that smelled of soap and steam and hot irons.

"Ta-da! It's the laundry," announced Xavier, opening the doors of a vast cupboard that spanned an entire wall. The cupboard was lined with immense shelves, piled high with snowy-white sheets. "Your parents will never find you down here!" he said. "And you can pretend you're in a ship's cabin! The housekeeper, Charlotte, doesn't start until nine. She'll never know."

Nell looked doubtfully at her proposed sleeping quarters. It was true that the shelves were as wide and as long as a small bed. But still, a cupboard!

"But I don't want to get you into trouble," she said.

"I won't tell my grandpa," he said. "If he knew you were here all on your own, he'd—"

"Tell the authorities," finished Nell.

"No!" Xavier looked shocked. "He'd say you must stay with us. But if the hotel found out, they'd go ballistic. He can't be harboring runaways or he'd lose *his* job. Look, did you say your friend worked at a place called Crown Couture?"

"Yes," said Nell.

"It's just—I know someone who might be able to help."

"Oh, Xav!" She had been right to follow him down into the tunnels. "When can we go?"

"I've got my shift here tomorrow morning, and then I've got to meet the others at Chez Ben Amor to break open Soutine's entrance," he said, thinking. "But we could use a lookout. Do you want to help? And then we can go after that."

After Xavier had gone, Nell lay awake for ages. If it was true that Pear had stolen something from a client at Crown Couture, then what had she stolen and why had she stolen it? Nell racked her brain, trying to remember if there had been any clues in the last letter she had received from Pear.

She yawned as tiredness engulfed her. The "bed" *was* comfortable. There was room to stretch out *or* curl up, and Xavier had left the door ajar, so she could glimpse a reassuring beam of light. A soft silence surrounded her, punctuated by the occasional tick of the vent and the sound of her breath, which gradually lengthened and deepened as sleep crept closer. Nell rearranged herself into her favorite position, like a stork with one leg straight and the other hooked up, foot to knee. It had been a tumultuous day. Things hadn't gone according to plan. But she had escaped Melinda and Gerald, and she had made friends.

Nell squeezed her eyes shut and conjured up her patch-work of Pear. Pear snuggled up to her in bed telling her stories. Pear tossing pancakes and getting one stuck on the ceiling. Pear trying to walk up the London Underground escalators when they were going down.

Tomorrow she was going to be a lookout. She would help Xav, and then he would help her. The thought filled her with hope. Maybe tomorrow she would find Pear.

ELEVEN

Wake up!" Someone was tugging at her. Light was invading her warm, cozy space. It was like being wrenched from a cocoon.

"Nell, listen!" It was Xavier, looking all sharp and snappy in his bellboy uniform. "Guess what?"

"What?" said Nell, forcing herself to sit up. She rubbed her eyes, swung her legs over the side of the shelf, and climbed down.

"I've asked around, and your parents didn't come back. In fact, it turns out they've bolted and left without paying the bill. A big one!"

"Uh-oh," said Nell.

"The boss is furious. The police were called and everything! Anyway, that means you can't be seen around, not unless you want the cops on to you. But don't worry, I've had a brain wave that will entirely solve everything!"

There was a pause while Nell's sleep-befuddled head tried to make sense of what Xavier had just said.

"Not the Pear problem," Xav said quickly, in case Nell jumped to the wrong conclusion. "Hopefully, we'll solve that later. You're short on cash, right? Well, my plan can kill two birds with one stone. You'll be in disguise and earn money at the same time."

Xav was carrying a plastic bag, and now he withdrew a crumpled scarlet uniform, identical to the one he was wearing. "Ta-da!"

It turned out that someone named Tomas Pinault had gone to visit his uncle up north. Nell was going to pretend to be him! It would be the perfect disguise. There were loads of bellboys scurrying around, explained Xav, and no one would notice one more.

"You'll make a ton of tips if you work hard," said Xav. Nell remembered the coins he had shown her yesterday, the ones that were going to be spent on a *chocolat Liégeois*. She beamed. She could've hugged him. Then doubt struck.

"But, Xav," she said, "I can't carry suitcases on my head or spin plates and twirl trays."

"You don't have to be able to do those things!" Xav

laughed. "It's mainly just carting around luggage and delivering newspapers and stuff." He thrust the uniform at her. "Make sure you tuck your hair under your cap."

Xavier waited outside while Nell dressed. The pants were too short and showed her ankles, and she had to breathe in to get the buttons done up on the jacket. She pulled the cap on, twisting her hair into a bundle and tucking it in.

"Aren't there any bell girls?" she asked when Xavier came back in and had nodded approvingly at her getup, even though she didn't look half as dashing as him. The brass buttons on the cuffs of the jacket winked as she rolled her clothes up and stuffed them into her bag.

"No! Everyone knows that."

"I didn't! Why not?"

"There just aren't," said Xavier as if that ended the matter. It was an extremely unsatisfying answer, thought Nell, who passionately believed that anything boys could do, girls could do just as well, if not better. She determined to do the job the very best she could. That would show them. No bell girls, indeed!

Nell had a brilliant morning. It was a million times better than being at school. You lurked by reception and waited for Monsieur Jacques to ring his bell, and when he did, you ran over and he sent you on an errand. Sometimes it was to deliver a neatly folded newspaper (they actually *ironed* them to get them perfectly smooth!) or purchase cigarettes or mail letters. More often than not, it was to cart luggage around, in or out of the hotel. She even got to walk a lady's dog around the block. It was a tiny little pompadoured thing, sporting a ridiculous-looking red vest studded with crystals. Whatever you did, the customer always gave you a tip, and by midmorning, her pockets were jangling with centimes and francs.

"Boy!" Nell jerked to attention. She had just deposited the last piece of luggage belonging to an elderly gentleman into a car waiting outside. Was that the first time Monsieur Jacques had called her or the second? She still hadn't got used to being called *boy*.

"Quick, quick, there's a baby in the Winter Gardens Café who needs minding for a minute or two; off you go."

Nell made her way to the café that was in a grand room off the lobby. How delightful it was with its overflowing bouquets of flowers, its glinting mirrors lining the walls and mint-green banquette seating. Waiters in black tailcoats flew about bearing trays piled high with silver coffee pots and fancy cakes. Around the tables sat beautiful ladies dressed in the latest fashions, chirruping and chattering like exotic birds. A lady in a pink-and-yellow feathered hat beckoned Nell over. "I need to make a phone call," she said to Nell. "Mind the baby for a minute, please." The baby boy beamed joyously at Nell. He had deliciously fat pink cheeks. In his hand he held on victoriously to a gooey chocolate éclair.

Nell sat next to the baby, who was propped up in a mountain of chintzy cushions, stabbing happily at his mouth with the éclair. A river of chocolate wended its way down his chin and dripped *plop, plop* onto the cushions.

"Oops," said Nell, taking a napkin from the table and dabbing the baby's chin. But the baby didn't like that. His mouth turned down and he started to whimper.

Nell wasn't used to babies. If he cried, she wouldn't know what to do. She stopped dabbing and tried not to worry about the chocolate river.

Madame Feather Hat had said a minute. But at least two minutes had gone by. Where was she? She scanned the room. It was then that she noticed two women on the other side of the café. Were they staring at her? Surely not. One was smoking a cigarette held in an extraordinarily long green cigarette holder. The other had a lorgnette, a pair of spectacles with a handle that she was holding up to her eyes. Nell glanced away and then looked back. The woman with the lorgnette was pointing in her direction. She wasn't imagining it.

By now the baby's cries had progressed to full-blown wails, and other people were starting to stare, too. Nell patted his hand and he quieted a bit. She looked back at the women. They were still staring. Suddenly, Nell felt a shiver of apprehension. Might the women be plainclothes police officers? What if they were on the lookout for Penelope Magnificent, accomplice to the Magnificents who had taken off and not paid their bill?

"Goodness, what *has* he done to you?" Madame Feather Hat was back, scooping the baby up and dropping a franc into Nell's hand. For a second, Nell thought the woman was talking about the baby.

"No, he—" she started, and then she stopped. Of course, it was she who was the he, and she must keep up the charade even if the women across the way were on to her. "Thank you, Madame. Have a good day."

Nell hurried out of the café. She could feel the eyes of the two women boring holes in her back. But when she turned to check, scanning the crowd for a cigarette holder and a lorgnette, she couldn't see them anywhere.

TWELVE

I think they were plainclothes police officers," said Nell as she and Xav negotiated their way across the busy Place de la Concorde, two flashes of scarlet in a sea of cars. It was now midday and they had finished their shifts. "I don't think the disguise fooled them for one minute."

"Nonsense," said Xav, pausing to roll up his pants. "How would they know? They were probably just two nosy busy-bodies. We get all sorts staying here."

They were on their way to Chez Ben Amor, Soutine's family patisserie, where they were going to break open the entrance that the mayor's Municipal Department had blocked. Xav wanted to walk via the Grands Boulevards so they could window-shop on the way. Printemps and

Galeries Lafayette were his favorites, he said, wonderful department stores selling anything your heart desired. But Nell begged to take the smaller roads. Remembering Xavier's maps, she wanted to show off her own orienteering skills.

"Please! I know the way," she pleaded.

"But you only arrived two days ago!" said Xavier.

"Just you watch!" retorted Nell, and she strode off, conjuring up pictures in her head of the maps she had pored over: Rue Cambon, Rue de la Victoire, Rue Saint-Lazare. Everything was where she knew it would be. And now here they were, smack-dab at the foot of the Rue des Martyrs.

It was a busy little street running steeply up a hill and bustling with proper shops selling all sorts of necessary things: buckets and brooms, fruits and vegetables, meats, cheeses, shoes. Nell sniffed appreciatively. The aroma of roast chicken wafted across the street from the butcher's rotisserie, and on the corner a man piled hot, sugary doughnuts into paper cones.

"How did you do that?" Xavier asked, looking impressed. He had taken off his jacket now and tied it around his waist, which gave him the air of a buccaneer, thought Nell.

"Test me!" she boasted. "I've learned all the streets."

"Rue des Cinq-Diamants," he tried.

"Just off Boulevard Auguste-Blanqui," answered Nell promptly.

"Rue Lamarck?"

Nell pictured the tangle of streets and steps in Montmartre. "Behind the Sacré-Cœur," she shot back. She was enjoying this. It was like being on a TV game show.

"You won't know this one. Rue de Ménilmontant." She could tell Xavier was desperate to trip her up. But it was easy. She'd been there yesterday. "Just around the corner from Passage Julien Lacroix!" she crowed.

"You're good," said Xav with undisguised admiration. "How do you know all this?"

"Pear," said Nell proudly.

"Well, you'd better come on one of my expeditions and help me do some mapping," he said. "The others are useless—they won't concentrate, but you'll be good."

Two small figures flitted across the street. "Xav! Nell! We've got the bolt cutters!"

It was the twins, dressed all in black as if they were cat burglars about to take part in a heist. Between them, they held a heavy-looking plastic bag. Their dad, they informed Nell, was a plumber and had all the tools. Xavier greeted them with kisses, once, twice on each cheek, and Nell followed suit, feeling very French.

Soutine was waiting for them at the entrance to Chez Ben Amor. He ushered them in and stood proudly while they drank in the splendor of the shop: the floor inlaid with green, gold, and burgundy tiles; the glass counters piled high with *ficelles*, baguettes, and *pain de campagne* on one side and éclairs, tarts, and gâteaux on the other; and the smiles of Soutine's parents, Monsieur and Madame Ben Amor, welcoming them in like long-lost friends.

"Those are *deblah*," said Soutine, pointing at a plate of golden pastries that looked like delicate flower blossoms, "and these are *Kaber Ellouz*. The best Tunisian pastries in the whole of Paris!"

"Take one!" said Madame Ben Amor, her gold bangles jangling as she passed around the sugary pastel-colored balls. Nell bit into hers. Mmmm, it was marzipan and roses all rolled into one.

"Xav," said Soutine, casting a disparaging look at Nell, "if you don't mind me asking, why have you brought her here?"

"Soutine!" said Paulette. "Don't be rude!"

"I'm going to be the lookout," said Nell, who didn't need Paulette to stick up for her. Soutine's prickliness was nothing compared to what she was used to. Besides, she wasn't doing this for Soutine. She was doing it for Xavier because he had promised to help her find Pear.

As the others clattered down the staircase to the cellar, Nell took her position in the doorway and gazed up and down the street. Nothing sinister seemed to be happening. There were no Municipal Department men parading around with badges. All she could see were ordinary shoppers going about their business. And it was a beautiful day. The sky blazed a deep blue and the leaves in the trees fluttered gently. Nell did as Xav had, rolling her pants up and pushing her sleeves above her elbows. She leaned against the doorjamb and tilted her face toward the warm sun.

Wouldn't it be marvelous if all of a sudden Pear just appeared, swinging her way down the street, her golden hair curling around her shoulders, her straw shopping bag dangling from her arm? Nell imagined leaping to her feet and rushing toward her, the embrace, the laughter, and the explanations that would follow.

People didn't just disappear into thin air. It wasn't possible. Unless they were kidnapped or killed. But why would someone want to kidnap Pear?

Nell scanned the street again for any signs of men with badges. A gaggle of small children emerged from the grocery store a few doors down, brandishing ice pops. A delivery van stopped over the way, and a young man leaped out and started transporting tinkling crates of bottles into the café on the corner. Two elderly ladies pulling wicker baskets on wheels ambled by and stopped to squeeze the apricots on a fruit stall.

No suspicious behavior. Unless . . .

Right at the top of the street, almost on the cusp of the hill, two figures had appeared, much too far away to see if they were sporting the dreaded badges.

Nell squinted. The figures were a bit blurry. Recently, she had wondered if she might need glasses. She had mentioned it to Melinda, but Melinda had just sneered and said there had never been any four-eyes in the Magnificent family and there weren't going to be any now. Nell narrowed her eyes because she had found that if you did that, things became a bit clearer. The two figures were getting closer. They were walking quite fast.

One was grasping an extraordinarily long cigarette holder.

The other was clutching a lorgnette.

They were the women who had been watching her in the hotel!

With a lurch, Nell abandoned her post and dashed to the top of the cellar steps.

"Are you in?" she shouted. They were detectives! They were coming to arrest her for the unpaid bill. She'd be dragged off to the police station, and she wouldn't be able to go with Xavier to find out more about Pear!

"Nearly!" Paulette shouted back.

"Are the Municipal Department people coming?" yelled Soutine.

"No, but . . ." It was too complicated to explain from here.

Nell broke off and dashed back to her post. The two women were within throwing distance now.

A wail came from inside the shop. "Asim! Soutine!"

Nell ran inside again, nearly colliding with Soutine's father.

"Look!" Madame Ben Amor was holding a baguette out to her husband. It looked like any old baguette. Tall and skinny with a golden crust.

"What is it? What's the matter, Nadia darling?"

"I'll tell you what the matter is," said the customer who was standing by Nadia's side. "I bought this baguette from you only an hour ago. When I got home, I found a speck of mold on it. By the time I got back, it looked like this!"

The customer grabbed the baguette from Nadia and

stuck it under Asim's nose. She jabbed at it with her finger. "See?"

Asim and Nell looked. This close, you couldn't miss it—tiny speckles of mold blooming on the loaf's end. Oh no, thought Nell. Was this the Thing that everyone was talking about?

Nadia wailed again. Soutine and the others, hearing the commotion, bounded up the stairs and crashed into the shop. "*Maman*, what is it?" said Soutine.

"It's started," said Nadia, and her voice was trembling.

"We'll stop it," said Asim purposefully, and he swiftly began to pick up one loaf after the other. "Soutine, help me. Anything with mold on it, put it in here. Let's separate it, keep it apart."

"Asim!" Nadia Ben Amor spoke sharply. "That won't do any good and you know it. What did that report say?"

"'From the sight of the first mold, it takes four hours until everything is contaminated,'" recited Soutine.

Nell felt sick. The sort of sick feeling you get when something awful is about to happen and you can't stop it. The Ben Amors' faces were tight with worry. A sense of foreboding hung over the shop.

"Well, what if they've gotten it wrong?" said Asim. "We have to try something, Nadia!"

"Papa's right," said Soutine, grabbing a box, and together, father and son started to methodically go through the bread, eyes scanning furiously for the tiniest specks of mold. To Nell, it seemed like every single loaf and pastry was going into the box. The mold thing seemed to be running wild.

"There are specks on everything, Papa!" said Soutine.

The bell rang as another customer entered the shop. "Now, look here," he said angrily, not seeming to notice that he had arrived in the middle of a crisis. He tipped half a dozen croissants onto the counter. "Mold on every one of them! I shall be taking my business elsewhere. Pain-tastique doesn't have these troubles, you know." Nell wanted to grab the man and push him back out of the shop. Couldn't he see what was happening?

"Sir," said Nadia, and Nell could see the effort it took for her to gather herself before she spoke, "we are sorry about that. We have done our utmost . . ."

"Oh, what's the point in saying sorry!" exploded Soutine. "It's not our fault, and he knows it!"

Xavier stepped forward and attempted to put an arm around Soutine's shoulders, but Soutine, rubbing his eyes with his fists, shook him off. In an instant, Nell forgave him all his prickliness. Anyone would be prickly if they'd had this hanging over their head. They must have dreaded it so much, and now it really was happening.

"I think it would be a good idea if everyone left," said Asim Ben Amor quietly, his shoulders drooping.

"Yes, go," said Soutine. He wouldn't meet their eyes. It was heartbreaking. "There's nothing anyone can do."

THIRTEEN

Nell and Xavier said goodbye to the twins and walked silently down the Rue des Martyrs. There was no sign of Cigarette Holder or Lorgnette. Perhaps she had imagined them, just like she had imagined Pear walking toward her down the street. All around them, the shops and stalls were in full swing, oblivious to the drama that had just taken place in Chez Ben Amor. Nell cast a sideways look at Xavier. She wanted to ask him if he was still going to take her to his friend, the one who might be able to help in her quest to find Pear. But his mouth was turned down and she could tell that all he was thinking about was Soutine.

"Did you hear that customer?" he said at last. "Telling Monsieur Ben Amor they were going to buy their bread from somewhere called Pain-tastique?"

Nell nodded.

"I don't understand it," said Xav. "The hotel has started ordering from them, too. And their stores are springing up all over the place! One opened in République yesterday and another one is coming to Clignancourt next week. But surely the Thing, whatever it is, will go there, too?"

"Mmm," said Nell.

Xavier sighed and stopped to admire the window display of an umbrella shop. There was a lovely Mary Poppins—style one with a parrot handle at the front. He turned to Nell, and his mood seemed to lighten a little. "It's not your worry. Sorry. Anyway, thanks for being the lookout. At least we managed to break open Soutine's entrance again. Now, I owe you a favor."

"They live down here," said Xav. He and Nell had jumped on the Métro at Pigalle and traveled five stops to Madeleine. Now they were making their way down a narrow street just off a busy square.

"Who lives down here?" asked Nell, hurrying to catch up. He hadn't offered any explanations about where he was taking her.

"My cousin and aunt. There she is. Neige!" Xav waved wildly and darted across the road toward a girl outside a grocery store. She was busy loading a large wicker basket with vegetables and somehow managing to read at the same time.

Nell stopped where she was. Red hair in braids. A blue dress and white tennis shoes. It was the girl who worked at Crown Couture! The one she had followed. The one who had shouted at her that Pear was a thief and then disappeared underground.

"Nell!" yelled Xavier. "Come on!"

Of course they were cousins. Who else had hair that color, blazing orange with gold tips at the ends?

Now Neige saw Nell, and her eyes widened in disbelief. "Xav, what are YOU doing with her?" she demanded.

Galvanized, Nell ran across the road to join them. "Is SHE your cousin?"

Xav, baffled, looked from one to the other. "Do you two know each other?"

And then they were both speaking at once. "She followed me—"

"She knew something—"

"She knocked me over! Ruined my copy of *Little Women*—"

"She said Pear was a thief!"

"Stop!" Xavier held up his hands like an umpire.

"Neige, can we come in to visit Aunt Sophie? Then Nell might understand."

Neige's apartment was above a *tabac*. She retrieved a key that was tucked down her sock and let them in. It was small with three rooms: a bedroom each for Neige and her mother and a tiny kitchen with just enough space for a table and two chairs.

"Xav's with me," called Neige as they entered. "And his friend Nell. Go and say hello," she said to them, "while I make the soup. *Potage Bonne Femme* for dinner today, *Maman.*"

"But—" Nell didn't want to say hello to Aunt Sophie; she wanted to talk to Neige.

Neige shook her head. "We will talk," she said firmly, "but only after you've said hello."

Nell trailed after Xav, following him into a bedroom. She saw right away that Aunt Sophie was ill. She was thin and frail, reminding her of a wounded sparrow she had once tried to rescue in the playground. She'd only wanted to pick it up and nurse it back to good health. But a teacher had shouted at her that birds were vermin and if she touched it there would be trouble.

"*Coucou, Tatie Sophie,*" said Xav, leaning in gently to kiss his aunt on both cheeks. Nell felt a rush of shame. She'd knocked Neige over and shouted at her. That wasn't a nice thing to do to someone who was caring for her sick mother. No wonder Neige had been angry.

"How's Papa?" Aunt Sophie asked Xavier. Her hand held his, her wrist tiny and delicate like the bone china that Melinda used for her Lapsang souchong tea.

"You wouldn't believe what he's made down in that boiler room of his now," started Xavier, launching into a description of a lamp made from candlesticks and copper piping, and all of a sudden Nell realized that Xavier's grandfather must be Michel, the man in the hotel basement who had made her hot chocolate on that first day. Of course! Those drawings she'd looked at had been Xav's maps. She couldn't believe she hadn't put two and two together before.

"And you are working at the Crillon, too? So they're taking girls now? Hurrah, at last!" Aunt Sophie smiled, taking in Nell's uniform and the coil of long brown hair that had escaped from the cap.

"Yes and no," Nell said, and they all laughed. She didn't want to say that she had really been a guest at the hotel. There was something about being in this apartment, so small and homely with Xav's cousin making soup out of nothing more than a handful of vegetables, and she sensed—she wasn't sure what—but it was something to do with hardship and struggle that was wholly different than anything she knew.

"*Maman.*" Neige stood in the doorway. She had tied a scarlet apron around her waist and was clutching a wooden spoon. She glanced at Nell, and now she had the same expression that she'd had in the atelier when she had appealed to the older woman. "Nell's trying to find someone who worked at Crown Couture. Perrine Chaumet."

Nell almost stopped breathing. She wanted to jump up and shake the whole story out of Neige. But she couldn't, not in front of Aunt Sophie.

"Perrine! The one who embroidered so beautifully?" asked her mother.

"Yes, her. Nell, do you want to help me with the soup?" In the kitchen, Neige gave Nell a carrot to chop. She had been reading again, her book propped up against the sink. Carefully, she marked her place with a potato peeling and set it to one side.

"What is it?" Nell tried to keep her voice low even though she felt like shouting. "This is what you were going to tell me yesterday, isn't it? Before Monsieur Crown came in and spoiled everything. I'm sorry I chased you. If I'd known about your mum, I wouldn't . . ." She trailed off. She really wasn't in the mood for chopping carrots.

Neige wiped her hands on a tea towel. Her gaze was serious. "Now you've seen *Maman*, do you understand why I can't do anything to jeopardize my job?"

"But you're only . . ." Neige looked too young to work anywhere. When she'd seen her at Crown Couture yesterday, Nell had assumed hers was a summer job—or a Saturday job. Some of the older girls at Summer's End boasted about their Saturday jobs, in shoe shops or boutiques. They liked to flaunt the jewelry and nail varnish they bought with their earnings.

"I'm fourteen," said Neige, taking the chopped carrot from Nell and adding it to the pan. "Old enough for an apprenticeship in France, even though I'd rather be at school . . . But anyway, Monsieur Crown didn't mean any harm. It's part of his artistic temperament."

Nell snorted. "But he was horrible to you! Does he know about Aunt Sophie?"

"Yes, of course he does. I only got the job because *Maman* worked there before she got sick. She'll be going back when she gets better." Neige gave the soup another stir. "The thing is, I don't mind Monsieur Crown's temper, but I do mind secrets." She looked straight at Nell. "Of course,

Mademoiselle Chaumet—I mean Pear, is that what you call her?—did work at Crown Couture. She was an embroiderer. A *brilliant* one. Any stitch, she could do it. Monsieur Crown used to say there was music in her needle and dancing in her thread."

This was what Nell wanted to hear! She allowed the words to sink in while Neige added water to the pot and then stirred; she unscrewed a small jar and sprinkled in some herbs.

"But she's not a thief?" asked Nell.

"I don't know," Neige said simply. "She was fired, that is for sure. They said she stole a brooch from one of the clients and was dismissed on the spot."

"But Pear would never steal anything!" protested Nell.

"The brooch was in her sewing case," said Neige matter-of-factly. "They said she had a grudge against that particular client."

"When was this?" asked Nell.

"I remember exactly when it was," said Neige, "because it was *Maman*'s birthday. January fifteenth. I had to leave work on time that day so I could collect a strawberry tart from the boulangerie on the way home."

January fifteenth. The last letter Nell had received was dated December fifteenth. And she'd had nothing since then.

"But why didn't anyone tell me this at Crown Couture?"

Neige lifted a spoonful of soup, blew on it, and tasted it. "You must understand, if word gets out that one of our seamstresses is a thief, then no one will come anymore to have their gowns made. Don't you see? It would destroy the reputation of the atelier."

"I don't give a fig about the atelier! Pear is no thief, and you'd better believe it," said Nell hotly. She clenched her fists tight.

"Suit yourself," said Neige. "You asked; I was only telling you."

"I'll prove it!" said Nell. "Just you wait."

A sense of burning injustice raged through her. Hot tears pricked at her eyes. But next door, Aunt Sophie was talking softly to Xavier. It wouldn't do to explode here. Slowly, she uncurled her fists and tried to let her chest relax.

"Do you recognize this?" She fished the wispy scrap of pale-green fabric out of her pocket, the one embroidered with blue birds and pink cherry blossoms. "How did you get that?" Neige stopped stirring, took the scrap of fabric, and ran her finger over it gently.

"I found it in her apartment," said Nell. "She wasn't there, but this was."

"This is what she was working on before she left!" said

Neige. "It was going to be an evening gown for someone—an actress, I think. But the order was canceled after Perrine left. Madame Josette was livid."

A wave of sadness washed over Nell. Now that Pear had disappeared, the gown would never be finished. What an exceptional gown it would have been, dancing with blue birds and cherry blossoms. She tucked the tiny wisp of fabric safely back into her pocket.

Neige ladled out the soup into a bowl and set it on a tray. Her eyes softened and she laid a hand on Nell's arm. "Look, your Pear really is very good. She's bound to be working for another couturier."

"Then I need to go around every single one until I find her!" said Nell.

"Tell you what, come and meet me during my lunch break tomorrow," said Neige, "and I'll write you a list of all the places you can try. Will that help?"

"Yes. Thank you," said Nell gratefully. Neige had turned out to be all right, after all.

FOURTEEN

For the second night running, Nell slept in the laundry room. And just as the day before, in the morning Xavier came to collect her, with croissants and orange juice to scarf down before their bellboy duties started.

It was a busy morning, and Monsieur Jacques's bell never seemed to stop pinging. First Nell delivered a mountain of pressed newspapers, then she carted pile after pile of luggage outside to waiting cars. And for a good half hour, she sat in the tiny office tucked away behind the desk and stuck stamps on letters.

"Boy!" Monsieur Jacques poked his head around the door, making Nell jump. "Have you got cotton wool in your ears? I've been ringing and ringing for you!" Nell leaped up in what she hoped was a boyish-looking way.

"Are they all stamped?" he asked, looking at the letters Nell had arranged in a teetering tower.

"Yes sir," said Nell, trying to give the same salute she'd seen Xav deliver, a sort of simultaneous half nod of the head, touch of the cap, and click of the heels. It had looked effortless when he did it, but when Nell tried, she got in a twist and nearly fell over her ankles.

"Stand up straight, boy!" snapped Monsieur Jacques. "And look sharp. I want you to run those over to the post office." He passed her a large square leather bag with a thick strap. "Been there before? You're new, aren't you?"

"Hmm," mumbled Nell, aware she might be on dangerous territory.

"Out of the door, turn left and left again. The post office is at the end of the street on the right."

"Very good, sir," said Nell, quickly sweeping the letters into the leather bag and pulling the strap over her head.

Outside, the sun beat down on the sidewalk. It was going to be a scorching day. Nell hopped down the steps of the hotel and turned left. She felt happy and hopeful. After her shift, she was going to collect the list from Neige and visit each and every couturier until she found Pear. What had Neige's words been? . . . *There was music in her needle and dancing in her thread.* Of course another couturier would have snapped her up! And then she would be able to find out why Pear had stopped writing, and if . . . if . . .

Nell chased the thought away. Pear would never abandon her.

It was such a beautiful day, and Nell was so deep in thought that she didn't even notice first one shadow, then another, fall across her path. So full was her head with pictures of Pear that, before she even knew what was happening, two figures had swooped silently on either side of her, grabbed her elbows, marched her swiftly down the street, and propelled her into a narrow passage.

"Let go! Ouch, you're hurting me!" Nell wriggled out of their grasp and backed away. But the hands clutched at her again, like tentacles, grasping and catching at her, fingers curling around her wrists, pulling her back. A push, a shove into the dark recess of a doorway. Two silhouetted figures looming side by side, blocking her escape.

Nell's heart thudded. It was the ladies who had been watching her in the café. The ones who had followed her to Soutine's shop.

"There's no point struggling," said Lorgnette.

"You aren't going anywhere," said Cigarette Holder.

"Is it about the hotel bill?" burst out Nell. "Look, I'm sorry! My parents can be forgetful. I can pay it." Furiously,

she dug in her pockets and started counting out her tips. Whatever happened, she mustn't be derailed in her search for Pear. "How much is it? Please don't arrest me. If I don't have it all now, I'll get you the rest tomorrow."

"We have absolutely no idea what you are talking about," said the one with the lorgnette coldly, holding her eyeglasses up and giving her captive a long, hard stare. Nell stared back, confused. What *did* they want then? Behind the bottle-thick glass, Lorgnette's eyes were magnified to huge proportions, cold and wet-looking, like a giant fish.

"Put your money away," said the one with the cigarette holder. "We just want to know where your parents are."

"Oh," said Nell, and then all in a rush she put her head down like a bull and tried to batter her way past them, but it was no good—they held fast, pinching her arms. "That hurts! Let me go!" she protested.

Neither of them replied. Instead, Cigarette Holder took a long, deep drag of her cigarette and blew a large puff of smoke straight into Nell's face, making her cough.

"I'm going to ask you one more time," said Lorgnette. "Where are your parents?"

"I don't know!" cried Nell. Should she tell them Melinda and Gerald had gone to Venice? If she did, they might leave

her alone. But what if they then told the authorities she'd been abandoned? Then she'd be carted off to a children's home and never find Pear.

"I'm sure they'll be back soon," she muttered, rubbing her arm where it had been pinched.

"They'd better be," said Cigarette Holder, blowing small circles of smoke: one, two, three, four, five, six, seven tiny puffs wafting out of her mouth and hovering in the air like the dots under the question marks that were exploding in Nell's head.

"The thing is—they've got something of ours," said Lorgnette softly.

"Something very important. And we want it back."

Lorgnette gave Nell's arm another hard pinch. She'd be black-and-blue at this rate.

"You tell them. Return IT or there will be trouble."

"Very big trouble."

Lorgnette lowered the eyeglasses and shoved her face close to Nell's. She smelled of extra-strong peppermints, the kind that make your mouth feel like it's on fire. "I'm sure they wouldn't want anything to HAPPEN to their darling daughter."

"I don't think they really—" started Nell.

"SHUT UP! I'm talking," shouted Lorgnette. Nell

flinched. She wouldn't be surprised if Lorgnette wasn't some sort of distant relative of the headmistress at school.

"What Mathilde is saying," said Cigarette Holder in a more normal voice, "is that if your parents don't return what's not theirs RIGHT AWAY, you"—she paused and exhaled two dragon lines of smoke out of her nostrils—"could be in danger."

"Do you understand, little girl?" demanded Lorgnette.

"Yes," said Nell, even though her mind was spinning and she didn't have a clue what they were talking about.

"Off you go, then." The fingers relinquished their grasp and pushed Nell out of the dark doorway and back onto the bright street.

Nell ran.

FIFTEEN

hey were horrible!" recounted Nell. "But I'm pretty sure they're not police detectives. They weren't interested in the unpaid bill at all. They just want my parents. They seem to think they've got something of theirs."

She and Xav were on their way to meet Neige to collect the list of couturiers that Pear might be working for. As they walked, they shared a baguette stuffed with ham.

"I feel terrible eating this," Xav said as he handed Nell a chunk. "It's from Pain-tastique. But Chef said he's had orders to change suppliers, and that's that." He took a big bite, chewing thoughtfully. "Sounds like your parents might have stolen something, if you believe what those ladies were saying. But what?"

"I don't have a clue!" said Nell. "Should I have told them they've gone to Venice?"

"Definitely not," said Xavier. "Not if they were trying to obtain information by force. Oh, look! What are the twins doing here?"

Outside Crown Couture, two outlandish figures were waiting for them, dressed to the nines in long, trailing dresses and white lace hats. The brims of the hats were so wide they obscured their faces.

"Hey!" said Paul, strutting up to meet them as if he were on a catwalk. "D'you think we look the part?"

"Who said you could help?" said Xavier.

"Oh, please!" said Paulette. "We saw Neige this morning when she was on her way to work, and she told us all about it. They're old bridesmaid's dresses." She gave an elegant twirl. "The lady in the apartment downstairs was throwing them out."

"Well, you're hardly incognito," said Nell. She remembered how Madame Valérie had reacted to her jeans and sweatshirt. These couture people were very particular about clothes.

"Speak for yourselves!" said Paul. Xav and Nell looked at each other, taking in their bellboy uniforms. Paul was quite right. They *did* look like an odd bunch. Paul snorted and then tripped over the train of his dress, and they all burst out laughing.

"See, he does sound like a pig when he laughs!" crowed Paulette, and they all laughed more, their noses running and their eyes watering as they took turns to see who could snort the loudest and the best.

"Stop it!" said Neige sternly as she slipped out of the Crown Couture door. "You're drawing attention to yourselves. I've got about a minute before Madame Josette notices I'm gone."

She thrust a slip of paper at Nell. "Here are the addresses. I'm pretty sure that's every couturier in Paris. If Perrine is still here, she'll be with one of them. Look, I'd better get back. Good luck."

There were at least twenty addresses on the list, all of them in and around the Rue du Faubourg Saint-Honoré. They decided to split up, Xavier working with Paulette, and Nell with Paul. At first, Nell was hopeful. At each fashion house, she politely inquired if a Perrine Chaumet happened to work there and showed them the slip of embroidery. She made a special effort to smile and be friendly. But every time, it was the same. A negative answer accompanied by a snooty stare.

When they had finally exhausted their list, they met up with Xav and Paulette, who'd had an equally fruitless search.

"Nell, maybe she doesn't *want* to be found," said Xav gently. They were squashed into Café Zinc, which Nell decided must have been the tiniest café in the whole world, with just enough space for a handful of chairs and tables. Behind the bar, Paul and Paulette entertained the owner by seeing how far they could walk on their hands.

"Are you saying you think she ran away?" said Nell.

"You don't think she's a thief, do you?"

"No, but . . . How well do you really know her? You say you were separated when you were seven . . ."

"Yes." Nell took a sip of her hot chocolate. Suddenly, it seemed to have taken on a bitter edge. What was Xav getting at?

"Well, think back. What happened? Why did she leave so suddenly?"

Nell *had* thought about it. Over and over, she had tried to dredge up exactly *what* had happened on that dreadful day. But however hard she tried, only a few wisps of memory floated back. There had been an argument, she knew that. Lots of shouting. And then Pear was gone, and she'd been sent to Summer's End.

"It's just," said Xav, "she's disappeared once. What's to say she hasn't chosen to disappear again?"

A swirl of unwelcome thoughts crowded Nell's head. Had Melinda told Pear to leave when Nell was seven? Or had Pear chosen to? The thought was like a needle scratching away at her skin.

"Perhaps you should go to the police," said Xavier. "Report her as missing?"

"No," said Nell with feeling. "She might be in hiding because of the brooch. What if we led the police to her? She'd never forgive me. We can't do that yet."

They were walking along the tunnel leading to the den when Soutine rushed out to meet them. "At last, where have you been?" He was shouting, his eyes flashing with a combination of anger and fear. Something was wrong.

"Look!" He pointed at a tangle of wire and tape on the tunnel floor.

"The tape recorder!" exclaimed Xav. It looked like someone had wrenched it from its hiding place and disemboweled it. "Who broke that?"

"It's worse than that—wait until you've seen what's happened," said Soutine.

"Not the den?" said Paulette. And then they were all

charging down the tunnel, Nell bringing up the rear, and even before she arrived, she could hear the dismayed cries.

"It's destroyed!"

"Someone's smashed it all up!"

"All our stuff is everywhere!"

"Beasts!"

It was a mess. The wooden crates that had served as seats were on their sides; the tin cups and plates had been swept off the table and scattered across the floor. On the shelves, everything was out of place and in a jumble. All the lovely order was gone. Now it looked like a junkyard.

"They want us out that bad," said Xavier, his voice trembling.

"It's that mayor and his stupid Municipal Department!" shouted Paul, wiping away an angry tear.

"Well, we're not going anywhere," said Soutine, picking up the crates and setting them upright.

It was a relief to find that nothing had been broken. Mostly, stuff had just been tipped out of boxes and swiped off shelves into a jumble on the floor. Nell retrieved chess pieces and put them back into their box, gathered up the books and replaced them on the bookshelf, picked up marbles and dropped them into their net bags.

"Look!" Paulette was waving a green cap in the air. "I don't remember this. Is it yours, Xav?"

"Nope," said Xavier. "Must be Soutine's."

"It's not mine," said Soutine shortly. He had given up tidying and was sitting, legs sprawled out in front of him, his back to the wall.

Nell, looking at the cap, felt a faint stab of recognition. She had seen it somewhere before.

"If it's not yours, then whose is it?" asked Paul, swiping it off Paulette's head and putting it on his own at a more rakish angle.

And then Nell remembered. The boy from Belleville had worn a green cap exactly like this one. What was his name? Emil! The one who had shown her Pear's apartment. He had worn it like Paul was wearing it now, just off-center, so the peak pointed to the side.

"Well, it's obvious, isn't it?" Soutine looked up angrily. "Whoever did this"—he swept his arm out to indicate the mess—"dropped their cap. It's a clue, isn't it? Wait until I find out who it belongs to!"

"Is there a name in it?" asked Xav. Paul took it off and examined the inside of the cap.

"Nope," he said.

"I met someone who has a cap like that," Nell ventured, reaching out and taking it. The fabric was soft, the way it gets after it has been washed multiple times.

"What do you mean, you met someone who has a cap like that?" Soutine asked suspiciously. "Do you have something to do with this?" He stood up and took a step toward her, his eyes glittering.

"Of course she doesn't," interrupted Xavier. "Do you, Nell?"

"No!" She turned the cap over in her hands. Hundreds of people must own caps like this. Just because it was green didn't mean it was Emil's. He had helped her. Surely he wouldn't be involved in something as destructive as this! Nevertheless, a lump sought its way into the back of her throat. Xavier and Soutine were regarding her intently.

"It doesn't mean it's his," she said. "I met him when I was looking for Pear. Near Rue Julien Lacroix."

"The Belleville bunch!" said Xavier. "What have they got against us?"

"We'll go and smash their den up. See how they like it!" said Soutine, his fists clenched. "How dare they?"

In an instant, Nell knew she had unleashed something bad. All Soutine's anxiety about the Thing and what it had done to Chez Ben Amor was going to be turned on the children from Belleville. And even if they had done this to the den—and they couldn't have, surely—what was the point in doing the same thing to them? It would go on and on and never end.

To make matters worse, Paul and Paulette were gleefully hopping about, circling each other, fists raised, like a pair of prize-winning boxers.

"We'll go underground," said Paul.

"Creep up and surprise them," said Paulette.

"Catch 'em red-handed!" crowed Paul. "Quick, look in the dress-up box." He dragged out a small trunk and started riffling through it. "We need fighting clothes."

"We'll take the Métro to Gambetta and get in via La Petite Ceinture," said Xavier. He had gathered up all his little maps, which had been strewn about, and held one aloft. "I only made this one last week. Now we can test it out."

Nell felt something heavy pressing down on her temples. She didn't *want* to go and bash up somebody's den. Especially someone who had helped her and might be able to help her again. Oh, *why* hadn't she just stayed quiet about Emil and his cap? But it was too late. They were already leaving, calling to her to follow. Well, it was done now. She would just have to go with them and at least try to stop this from turning into a full-blown battle.

SIXTEEN

L a Petite Ceinture was an abandoned railroad that had not been in operation since the 1930s. As Nell clung to a lamppost and peered over the high wall, she found it hard to imagine that the deserted tracks below had once been busy with steam engines. Now it was all overgrown brambles and rotting wooden timbers, a place to wander and hide, and in its tunnels, Xavier promised, access to the underground.

Nell navigated her way from the lamppost to the wall and, chest thumping, threw herself down into the weeds below. For a minute, the force of her landing sent spirals of pain up and down her legs. Gingerly, she stretched first one leg, then the other, and waited for the pain to subside. Now Paul and Paulette followed, crawling down the wall like spiders, somehow finding invisible footholds and landing with far more grace. The railroad had an otherworldly feel to it, narrow and enclosed, with greenery-choked walls and an eerie light that made it look like a fairy glen. Nell stood up and looked both ways. Ahead of her, the tracks stretched away, starting to make the slow ascent aboveground. In the other direction lay the gaping black mouth of the tunnel.

Xavier said they should save their flashlight batteries, so they ventured into the tunnel using only the dwindling daylight to navigate by. Nell squinted ahead, hoping for a pinprick of light to cheer her on. But it was black as night.

"Can we switch our flashlights on now, Xav?" she asked. They had just rounded a bend, and the comforting shaft of light that had tailed them for the last ten minutes had almost dropped away. She could barely see where she was putting her feet.

"Nope, not yet," replied Xavier. Through the gloom, Nell could just make out his familiar shape, feeling his way along the wall of the tunnel. She could sense his excitement, not for the impending fight, but for the tunnels and his knowledge, a knowledge that must be constantly expanding as he explored more and more of this underground paradise.

Nothing could happen. Xav was ahead and the others

were behind. Carefully, she reached out so her own fingers grazed the wall, and for a minute, the solidity of the cold brick steadied her. *Be brave, Nell,* she told herself. It's only the dark.

At last, Xav flicked on his flashlight, illuminating three steps leading down to a small door. "That'll take us directly to Rue des Couronnes," he said, fishing out his map. "The Belleville den is really close. Go quietly. They could be waiting."

"We'll ambush them!" whispered Paulette.

"We'll make 'em pay!" agreed Paul.

"We'll grab 'em and get the truth out of them," said Soutine, and they all nodded enthusiastically, except Nell.

"But what if it's not Emil's cap!" she said. But no one was listening. Instead, they were busily clicking on their flashlights and making their way down the steps and through the door in the wall.

"Let's run," Xavier called. "Take them by surprise." And so they did, the *slap, slap* of their shoes echoing around the tunnel walls—Xav first, because his flashlight had the longest reach, then the twins, then Soutine. Nell brought up the rear. She was a good runner, but she wasn't used to running underground.

"Oh!" Xavier's shocked voice floated back down the

passage to her. They must have found the den. Xav was right—it hadn't been far.

"What is it?" she whispered, catching up. They were standing in a huddle, gazing into the mouth of a small cavern. It was the Belleville den. And it had been smashed up even worse than their own.

A table lay on its side with its legs torn off; a set of chairs looked as though a giant fist had punched right through their wicker seats; broken crockery littered the floor; books, comics, and playing cards had been shredded into tiny pieces and scattered everywhere. Nell searched for the word you would use to describe a scene like this. Like a bomb or an explosion.

Carnage! That's what it was.

"What do we do now?" Paul asked, his voice small. The twins' fists were no longer clenched. Soutine's shoulders had slumped even farther. Xavier seemed at a loss for words.

"Well, I know what I'm going to do," said Nell. She was still clutching the cap. "I'm going to give this back to Emil." She had to see him. She should have gone back earlier. There might be something—anything—he had forgotten to tell her about Pear. "And don't you want to know what happened down here?"

"Who goes there?" A voice shot out at them, exploding the silence, making them jump and Paul scream.

The bright beam of a flashlight stabbed out at them, far stronger than their own, catching them in its light like frozen mice.

Nell squinted. Behind the light was . . . a uniform, the gleam of a badge.

"Run!" yelled Xavier.

And they did, turning and stumbling down the passageway, away from the voice and the light. But the ground was uneven, and this part of the tunnel was so narrow that running as fast as you can in single file is hard, especially if someone up ahead trips, gets up, and trips again—was it Paul or Paulette? Nell didn't know, but it was enough to slow her down, allow the footsteps that were thundering behind to close the gap, and enable a hand to reach out and grab her, drag her back.

"Let her go!" It was Xavier. "What are you doing? She's got nothing to do with this!" Nell struggled to twist out of the man's grasp, but he held fast, marching her back, past the destroyed cavern and to a rope ladder clinging to the wall.

"Up there," he ordered, shining the flashlight into her face. "You too." He prodded Xav roughly. "Yves," he yelled, "I'm sending two tunnel rats up." His bulk filled the narrow tunnel—there was no hope of escape.

Nell had barely reached the top rung when large hands reached down, hoisted her up, and then unceremoniously dropped her on the floor. She scrambled to her feet just in time to see Xav get the same treatment.

Another Municipal Department man was looming over them. "How many more of you are down there?" he barked. "I thought we'd gotten rid of you all."

"You'll never catch them," said Xav. "They're too fast for you."

"I suggest you watch your mouth," the man said, his eyes roving over them, taking in their bellboy uniforms. "Hotel de Crillon, eh?" He regarded Nell. She didn't have her cap on, and her hair was trailing over her shoulders. "Take girls now, do they? Come on, names and addresses." He dug in his pocket for a notepad and pencil. "The mayor has been crystal clear about the new rules. No children in the tunnels. Your parents will be notified about this."

Nell's heart flew into her throat. This was it. She was about to be found out.

"I'm Xavier Bonnet," said Xav. "I live in the Crillon with my granddad, Michel Bonnet, and this is my cousin, Neige."

Nell felt a whoosh of relief. "I live above the *tabac*," she said. Would Neige mind? Xav must think she wouldn't.

"Seventeen Rue Moutarde," added Xav.

"She can speak for herself, can't she?" the Municipal Department man interrupted.

"My mum is Sophie Bonnet," said Nell. Her hand stretched out and found Xav's, gave it a grateful squeeze. "But please don't bother her—she's sick, and I don't want her to worry."

"Just this once, then. Makes a change to have a bit of cooperation," said the Municipal Department man, flipping his notebook shut. "Now, get out. Scoot." He nodded to a flight of steps leading to an open manhole. Light from the street flooded in. "And don't come back."

Outside, Nell recognized where she was immediately. She was at the top of Passage Julien Lacroix, steep and stepped, with the railings wobbling their way down the hill and dozens of children playing. And there was Emil, minus his cap, chewing gum and blowing the biggest bubble she had ever seen. His eyes met hers, and the bubble snapped.

"Emil!" she said, and then before she could stop him, Xav had marched over and started prodding him in the chest.

"Hey! What's that for?" protested Emil.

"Lost your cap, have you?"

"What's it to you if I have?" said Emil. "You the cap police?"

"You trashed our den," said Xav. His fists were up now.

"Xav," said Nell, "stop it!"

But Emil's eyes had already narrowed. "Are you the Concorde kids?" he asked. "The ones whose headquarters are under the Crillon?"

"Yeah!" said Xav.

"Well, you got what was coming to you! You smashed our den first!"

Xav's fists dropped back to his sides. His mouth hung open. "We did not."

"Jean's uncle works for the Municipal Department," said Emil. "He *told* us you were caught red-handed! Said we should pay you back."

"What?" said Nell. What was Emil talking about?

"Told us where your headquarters were, so we went and done it. Didn't break nothing, though—"

"Except the tape machine!" cut in Xav.

"Well," said Emil, having the grace to look embarrassed, "it was the only way to stop them barking dogs. But we didn't break nothing else, not like what you did to ours. Just jumbled stuff about a bit, tipped it on the floor." He looked at them defiantly as if daring them to suggest otherwise.

"Oh! Don't you see?" burst out Nell in exasperation as everything became clear. "That's what the Municipal Department is trying to do! Turn you all against one another. They're making you do their work for them. So you're driving one another out!"

Xav and Emil both looked at her, then looked at each other. She could see realization slowly creeping into their eyes.

"You should all be standing together. Fighting *them*, not one another."

Emil's face scrunched into a knot, and he thumped the wall with his fist. "I *knew* it wasn't right. It didn't *feel* right," he said angrily. He held out a hand to Xav. "Sorry?"

"'S OK," said Xav. "Sorry for your den, too. Even though we had nothing to do with it."

"Good thing you turned up," Emil said to Nell. "Remember my sister? Colette? When she came back from work that day, she wasn't happy. Told me I shoulda given you the letters. Said she woulda given them to you herself if she wasn't in such a tizzy about her first day at work. She's at *Le Monde*," he said proudly to Xav. "Gonna be a famous journalist."

"What letters?" asked Nell. Her whole body had started tingling.

"All the stuff clogging up your friend's pigeonhole. I woulda come and told you if I knew where you lived. Come."

Nell and Xav followed Emil down the street and into the alley. Just as before, they heaved themselves onto the trash cans, scrambled over the wall, and slithered down to the ground on the other side.

"Here!" Emil stood just inside the entrance to the block. He was pointing to a series of pigeonholes, each with a number on it. Reaching into one of them, he drew out a bundle of letters and passed them to Nell. The cream-colored envelopes were smooth in her hands. She riffled through them. Nine were ones she had sent to Pear, unopened. The tenth was addressed to her at Summer's End. Except her name and the address had been scrawled out and replaced with a strident message in red ink.

RETURN TO SENDER

School had sent the letter back! Why would they do that? She turned the letter over and read the message on the back with another jolt.

We have been instructed that you are no longer to correspond with Penelope Magnificent. All future correspondence will be destroyed.

Surely that was illegal? What was wrong with Pear writing to her? It made no sense. Had Melinda and Gerald made them do that? Nell tore the letter open. Her fingers were trembling. It was the shortest letter of Pear's she had ever received.

January 15

Darling Nell,

Everything was in place. I was going to come for you. But something has happened and I need to set it right. Do not lose faith. We will be together and the truth will come out.

Your dearest friend,

Pear

"The date!" Nell stabbed her finger at it and turned to Xav. "The fifteenth of January. Aunt Sophie's birthday. That was the exact same day that Pear was fired!"

SEVENTEEN

"Wait!" Xav and Nell stopped and turned. They were on their way back to the Métro because Xav didn't think it was safe yet to go underground. Emil bounded down the steps after them, his cap firmly back on his head. "I just thought . . . We could ask my sister to do a bit of nosing around. All of them journalists at *Le Monde* have . . . what did she call them? Contacts! She can ask around, see if they've heard anything about your missing friend."

"That would be good," said Nell. "Wouldn't it, Xav?"

Xav nodded, but he wasn't really listening. He was transfixed by a window display boasting sequins and buttons and ribbons, masses of them—tartan ones, spotty ones, grosgrain, satin, and ruffled ones. MARIE'S MERCERIE read the sign above the door.

A haberdashery! An idea bloomed in Nell's head. Without stopping to explain, she pushed the door of the shop open and stepped inside, beckoning Emil and Xav to follow. It was packed with sewing things: tiny scissors displayed in leather cases, spools of thread in every color of the rainbow, fringes, tassels, and all sorts of trimmings. On one side of the counter, a bunch of feather boas fluttered, on the other side sat a wooden box piled high with appliqués: strawberries, flowers, peace-and-love signs. 25 CENTIMES EACH read the price tag.

A woman wearing a caftan and perfectly penciled eyebrows wafted out from behind the counter. Huge gold hoops dangled from her ears. "The strawberry one's nice, isn't it?" she said, seeing Nell admiring it. It was nice. It was just the right size to patch over the hole in her favorite jeans.

"Yes," said Nell, digging in her pocket for twenty-five centimes and waiting while the lady rang up the price on the cash register and then tucked the appliqué into a little wax paper bag and slid it over the counter to her. "I've come to ask about a friend of mine. She's called Perrine. She used to live around the corner. She's an embroiderer, so she might have come in here to buy stuff. Have you seen her?"

Nell was glad she'd made the purchase. The lady was listening properly, looking like she wanted to help.

"Can you give me her surname? So I can check my invoices?"

"Chaumet," offered Nell. Her knees had gone a little weak.

There was a pause while the lady flicked through a small notebook covered in red velvet.

"Ahh!" She clapped her hands. "I know exactly who you mean. But I haven't seen her for a couple of weeks."

"A couple of weeks!" said Nell. Thankfully, there was a little chair by the door because all of a sudden she felt the need to sit down. This was an improvement on six months. "What did she say? Where was she living? What did she buy?"

"That's a lot of questions!" The lady laughed. "But I'm afraid I can only answer the last one. She was a regular customer of mine, but business was always on a professional level. No gossip, I'm afraid."

"Well, what *did* she buy?" asked Xavier. He had draped an emerald-green feather boa around his shoulders. Emil picked up a button from a small dish and flicked it so it landed, *ping*, on the counter.

"Thread," said the lady, giving Emil a stern but not unfriendly look. "Silk. Now what colors were they? Oh, I remember, that lovely kingfisher blue . . . and the rose pink. Said she was making something for a friend."

Nell felt as though she couldn't breathe. Her hand went to her pocket, fumbled for the wisp of fabric.

"Were they these colors?"

"Yes!" The lady nodded, her elegant eyebrows shooting up.

"If she comes back," Emil butted in helpfully, "can you come and tell me? I'm usually hanging around at the top of the street."

"It would be my pleasure," said the lady.

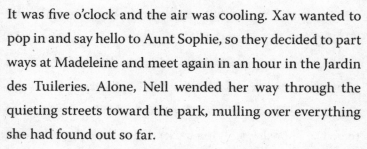

It was five o'clock and the air was cooling. Xav wanted to pop in and say hello to Aunt Sophie, so they decided to part ways at Madeleine and meet again in an hour in the Jardin des Tuileries. Alone, Nell wended her way through the quieting streets toward the park, mulling over everything she had found out so far.

Where was Pear? What "truth" had she been writing about in the letter? The truth that she was not a thief? Or something else? Nell ran her fingers along the sharp corner of the letter nestled in her pocket. She pictured the stack of unread letters in the pigeonhole. Pear *hadn't* ignored them. She'd hadn't even received them.

Best of all, she was still in Paris. Sewing something for "a friend."

"Pssst!" A sharp hiss stopped Nell in her tracks.

Where was that coming from? She peered inside the café she was passing, but the interior was too dark to see anything. She carried on.

"Pssst!" The hissing sound came again. Louder this time—and angry. Nell stopped and glanced back. It had come from the café. Something fluttered in the dark. It might have been a hand beckoning. Or a long silk scarf whipped by the breeze.

An unpleasant thought struck her. Cigarette Holder and Lorgnette. Were they still stalking her? Abruptly, she moved on.

"Penelope!" A razor-sharp whisper shot up the street after her, and even though a voice in her head started to yell *Get out, run away, pretend you didn't hear,* her feet started to do the opposite, walking back toward the café. *What are you doing? Stop, Nell! Turn around!* But her feet ignored her, taking her inside.

It took a minute for her eyes to adjust to the gloom. And then, there they were, Melinda and Gerald, sitting at a table hidden in a dark space behind the door. Nell froze. In an instant, the dread that followed her around in England was back. What were they doing here? Had they come back for her? But they were supposed to be in Venice!

To make matters worse, they looked like they were in a spy film, with large sunglasses covering half their faces and enormous fur hats pulled low even though it was summer outside.

It was almost funny.

Except it wasn't. It was horrible. Had they actually been in Paris this whole time?

"Sit down!" It wasn't a request; it was an order. Nell sat. She put her hand in her pocket and grasped hold of the letter for strength. Her whole body had gone all trembly. She hoped it didn't show.

"What on earth are you wearing?" Melinda was eyeing Nell's bellboy uniform with distaste.

"What are YOU wearing?" Nell shot back angrily. She'd forgotten how tormented her parents made her feel. "Where have you been? I thought you went to Venice!"

"Keep your voice down," hissed Gerald.

"For your information, we never intended to go to Venice, Penelope. We need to get back to London. But we can't without our passports. They're in my bag."

Despite the sunglasses, Nell could feel the icy chill of her mother's gaze.

"We've been looking and looking for you," muttered Gerald. "What have you been playing at?"

"But I've been at the hotel the entire time," protested Nell. "You could've just come and gotten me."

"We couldn't," snapped Melinda. "For reasons you do not need to know."

"What reasons? You never tell me anything."

"Just listen to your mother, will you?" interrupted Gerald. A trickle of sweat emerged from under his fur hat and snaked its way down his forehead.

"*Where* is my bag?" said Melinda, lowering her sunglasses and looking hard at Nell.

"What bag?" said Nell. Oh, why had she taken it? Stupid bag. It was a curse.

"You know very well which bag I am talking about," snapped her mother.

"Didn't see it," said Nell. She stared back at Melinda, trying to make her eyes go innocent and wide.

"What do you mean, you didn't see it? I left it in the ladies' room at the Crillon! I said to Gerald, 'It's OK, Penelope will bring it.' We were waiting for you in the taxi! Why didn't you come?"

"Oh, who cares about the bag?" Nell burst out. She couldn't stand it anymore. She pulled out the letter and threw it on the table. "Why wasn't Pear allowed to write to me? It wasn't affecting you."

"Where did you get this?" Melinda snatched the letter up and peered at it. "Oh, save me," she said to Gerald. "Will the child ever stop having this fixation with Pear?"

"You *must* know something! Like where she might be?" said Nell.

"Forget her," said Melinda. "I told you she is bad news. The bag—"

"Not getting it," said Nell stubbornly. "And anyway, what if I tell the hotel you are still in Paris? I'm sure the police would love to talk to you about the unpaid bill."

Melinda's face darkened. And then something clicked behind her eyes. "Bring me the bag and then I'll tell you what has happened to your precious Pear."

"You DO know something."

"Hush!" said Gerald.

"Tell me now."

"Doesn't work like that," snapped Melinda.

Nell stood up. "How do I know you're telling me the truth?"

"Just—get—the—bag." Melinda spoke deliberately

slowly. It was a manner of speaking that Nell detested and that Melinda deployed when she was determined to get her own way. "It will be in the hotel somewhere. Find it. And don't speak to anyone else about it. Understood?"

"All right," said Nell. She didn't have a choice. She had to do it.

"Meet us at Gare du Nord, Platform Two, Monday at ten o'clock. Do you have a watch?" said Gerald, drumming his fingers on the table.

"Yes," said Nell. It was Friday today. That gave her three days.

"And don't come in that ridiculous outfit," added Melinda. "This is serious, Penelope. Dead serious. If anything goes wrong, believe me, we will hold you person- ally responsible."

"Now, go." Gerald fluttered his fingers at Nell. "And we'll see you on Monday. With the bag."

Nell half walked, half ran back to the hotel. It was only half past five. She'd get the bag now and then meet Xavier afterward. But as she approached the boiler room, she heard Michel whistling. He must be tinkering with his stuff. He broke into a hum.

Uh-oh. He mustn't see her. Xav had explained what

would happen if he did. He was the sort of person who wouldn't be able to resist helping her. But if the hotel found out that he had helped or harbored a runaway, he'd lose his job.

Quickly, Nell crept past the boiler room and along the passage. In the laundry room, she delivered a swift kick to a neatly stacked pile of metal buckets, wincing as they crashed to the floor. In a flash, she leaped out into the corridor and concealed herself behind one of the big dressers. Immediately, Michel bustled out of the boiler room and into the laundry room to investigate. There was a clatter as she heard him start to tidy up.

Light on her feet, Nell raced back to the boiler room, heaved the cover off the manhole, and launched herself down the steps. Just in time, she remembered to reach up and drag the cover back over the hole. It clanged noisily. And then everything went utterly black.

Nell froze. The flashlights in the jam jars below weren't on! Quickly, she reached into her pocket for the flashlight she still had from the morning's expedition. It wasn't in the pocket with the letter. Ah, here it was in the other one, nestled against the scrap of fabric. Her fingers closed gratefully around the smooth plastic, found the switch, and clicked it on.

The light was weak, but it was enough. *It's not really dark, Nell,* she reassured herself as she climbed carefully down. All she had to do was get to the bottom, walk a short distance along the passage, and retrieve the bag from where she had hidden it. With the flashlight, she could do it. She knew she could.

She didn't have to go very far until she came to the spot where she had left the bag. She could clearly see the loose stone that she had wedged in to cover its hiding place. Pulling out the stone, she reached in, found what she was looking for, and pulled it out. The diamond clasp winked and gleamed in the weak light of the flashlight. But then the frail beam started to flicker. A small splutter. The light grew faint. And fainter. A last gasp. And then no light at all.

Nell let out a little sob. She couldn't see anything. She could feel her hands and feet and arms and legs, but she couldn't separate herself from the blackness surrounding her. "No," she moaned—she couldn't help it. "No."

The panic was sudden and insistent, clutching at her throat, not letting her go. This was it. She was going to drown in the dark, be sucked into the never-ending blackness where all thought and reason disappeared and only a kind of violent fear remained.

"Help," she called feebly. Nothing.

Her legs felt like jelly. She crouched down, panic coursing through her in great unruly waves. Who could survive what she was feeling now? If she stayed where she was, she would probably die. She needed the others. She needed them, and their flashlights, to rescue her.

"Help!" Nothing again. All she could hear were her own frantic attempts at deep breathing, a distant drip, and the faint rumble of the Métro or the traffic above.

With an enormous effort, she put her hand in her pocket. Felt for the little scrap of fabric that belonged to Pear. It was so fragile and slippery, and yet she could feel the stitches, stitches that made pictures of cherry blossoms and birds, grounding her somehow, giving her strength.

She told herself: *You are* here. *You are Nell. A living, breathing thing. You are separate. The dark is not going to swallow you up. Breathe. Breathe. Breathe.*

Nell slipped the bag over her wrist and dropped forward onto her knees. She planted both hands on the ground. *You can do it, Nell,* she said to herself. *You can do it. Pear would say you can.*

The ground felt solid. She tried to will some of that solidity up through her hands into her body. *Move, Nell, move! You've got to get out with the bag. It's your ticket to Pear.*

She imagined the irrational part of her brain trying to stamp down the rational part. With every ounce of concentration, she fought to reverse it. The dark couldn't kill her. She wouldn't let it. Slowly, she started to crawl. The bag, looped around her wrist, dragged alongside her, the chain making a horrible rasping noise matching the ragged sound of her breath.

"Come on, Nell, come on. Keep going, keep going!" It had taken seconds to get from the ladder to the hiding place. The same journey seemed to be taking forever to get back. The rough stone of the tunnel floor grazed the palms of her hands, and she could feel the holes tearing in the knees of her pants, which were growing more and more ragged as she crawled along.

At last, the floor became less rough, less littered with small stones. Now it felt smoother, sandier. Tentatively, Nell lifted a hand and reached out her arm. Yes, the walls of the passageway had opened up. She had reached the little cavern at the bottom of the steps. "You're almost there, Nell." And then, yes! Her hand made contact with the cold metal of the ladder. And even though it was black as night, Nell felt victory sweep through her. Here was the ladder; here was the bag, the cavern, the passageway, her broken flashlight. Here was the blackness, and here was she. Together but separate. Indistinct but distinct.

Up the ladder she went, step by step, and all of a sudden she was no longer running away from the dark. She wasn't scared anymore. The worst hadn't happened. She was the bravest, the strongest she had ever been.

A sliver of light appeared above her, a silhouette filling the hole and a hand, friendly this time, reaching down.

"Nell! What are you doing down there? It's way past six o'clock! I waited ages for you in the Tuileries!"

It was Xavier.

She had never, ever been so happy to see her friend.

EIGHTEEN

The coast was clear. Xav said his granddad was safely upstairs in their attic rooms. In the warm glow of the boiler room, Nell threw Melinda's bag onto the floor.

"She loves this bag so much," she said, "she'll do anything to get it."

Xavier picked up the bag, turned it over in his hands. "She loves it? It's nice, but . . . is that really why your parents want it so much?"

"Yes! It's her be-all and end-all," said Nell. She didn't think Xavier had quite grasped what her parents were like. "She loves it more than me!"

"It must be more than that . . ." he said.

"Well, she *said* it's because it's got the passports in it," Nell conceded. "Which they need to get back to London."

But Xavier was shaking his head. "You've forgotten something, Nell. Remember! *Your parents have something that isn't theirs.*"

Nell looked at Xav. And the shoe dropped. "Cigarette Holder and Lorgnette!"

Nell grabbed the bag again, tipping the contents onto the floor.

They stared at the small mound of stuff. If this was the treasure, it didn't look like much of a haul. A lipstick in a bullet-shaped case. A white handkerchief with a curly *M* embroidered in one corner. A small gold purse. A diary full of messy scribbles.

Nell peered into the now-empty bag. There was a zippered compartment inside. Unzipping it, she retrieved three passports. Hers, Melinda's, and Gerald's. Tucked into those were a couple of one-hundred-franc notes. Xavier whistled.

"Is there really nothing else?" he asked.

Nell dug her hand deeper into the zippered part. Something crackled. She felt for another opening with her fingers. Nothing. But there *was* something in there, she was sure of it.

"Can you feel that?" She passed the bag to Xavier. He dug his hand in. Prodded around.

"Scissors," he said. He rummaged around on Michel's work bench, found a pair. "I think they've sewn something into the lining."

Nell watched while Xavier carefully drew the sharp blade of the scissors along the turquoise-colored silk. She didn't know Melinda could sew. She must have been desperate to hide whatever was inside. There was a tearing sound. Xav dug his hand in again. Felt around. Drew something crackly out. A sheet of paper folded around something else.

He handed it to Nell, and very carefully she unfolded it.

"What in Napoleon's name is that?" asked Xavier. Tucked inside the paper was a clear plastic dish. It was about the size of a ginger cookie. It had a lid. And on the lid was a label. s13.

"I don't know," said Nell. It looked a bit like something you'd find in the science lab at school.

She examined the paper the dish had been wrapped in. It was covered in a sort of writing that made no sense: squiggles and symbols, loops and circles, curls and dots.

"It's gobbledygook!" said Nell. She didn't know the French for it, so she said it in English.

"What's gobbledygook?"

Nell burst out laughing as Xavier tried to get his tongue around the unfamiliar word.

"It means nonsense," she explained. "You can't make head or tail of it." She stopped laughing. "But it's not funny. It's *sinister*."

"Don't worry, Nell, we've got the whole weekend to find out what they're up to," said Xav.

Deep inside of Nell, a little flame of hope flickered. Perhaps this was the key that would lead her closer to Pear!

The next day was Saturday, and they didn't have to put their uniforms on because, on the weekend, another group of bellboys took over, the ones who would be there permanently starting in September when Xavier and the other summer workers went back to school.

It was a stroke of luck, Nell thought, pulling on her jeans and sweatshirt and stuffing the jacket and pants with their great raggedy holes into her bag. Monsieur Jacques would not have been happy with the state of her uniform at all.

They swiped croissants in the kitchen and then headed down to the tunnels and the den. Xavier showed Nell where the spare batteries were kept. She took a handful and put them safely in her pocket, feeling a glow of pride because she knew that if she lost them or used them up, and she was plunged into darkness again, the world would not end.

When the twins arrived, Nell laid the sheet of gobble-dygook on the ground, and they all sat munching their croissants and studying it.

"We've got two days until I hand it over," she said.

"Two days to find out what this funny business is all about," added Xav.

"Is it code?" Paul asked.

"I hope not," said Nell, who disliked reading stories that involved cracking codes. It always meant a lot of brain racking, and more often than not, the clues made no sense.

"Maybe your parents are witches, and it's a magic spell!" said Paul.

"Magic isn't real, dummy. S thirteen. I wonder what that means," said Paulette, picking up the dish and starting to open it.

"Don't!" yelped Nell so loud that Paulette jumped.

"Why not?"

"I don't know," admitted Nell. "But something just doesn't feel right."

"What's that, then?" said Paulette. She had turned her attention to the paper and was pointing at something in the corner, almost obscured by the gobbledygook scrawled on top of it. Nell hadn't noticed it before, but now she saw that the mark Paulette was pointing to looked like some sort of stamp. She picked up the paper and peered at it. A tiny circle with the initials *VH* inside.

"VH?" said Xavier. "What's that mean?"

"Vera Haricot." Paulette giggled.

"The lady who lives in the apartment next door," explained Paul when the others looked confused. "She's always shouting at us to tiptoe down the stairs."

There was a clatter, and Soutine skidded into the cave.

"I've found something odd, something not quite right," he said. "We've been staying with my cousin in the eighteenth. We were down in the tunnels this morning playing hide-and-seek, and we got a bit lost and . . . Well, I think you should see it. I'm not exactly sure how to get back there, though. Xav, do you have your maps? And, Paulette, bring the camera!"

It took nearly an hour to get there. They got lost once or twice, and Xavier made them all be quiet while he dug his map out of his pocket and examined it. But eventually they found themselves in a large, sandy-floored chamber. "We're under the eighteenth, Soutine. Where now?" said Xav. The eighteenth was the postal code for an area in the north of the city called Clignancourt.

"I don't recognize it," said Soutine. "I didn't come down

this way, but . . ." He sniffed, sniffed again, and nodded. "Can't you smell it?"

Nell sifted through the layers of smells wafting around her: the lemony pine of Paul, who had been liberal with his mum's scent that morning, the butterscotch of the candies that Paulette had shared earlier, the dust, hot in the beam of the flashlights, the old cave smell that never seemed to go away.

But . . . was there something else, too? She sniffed again. It was warm and yeasty. It was . . .

"Bread!" said Soutine.

"We must be below a boulangerie," said Xavier.

"Just you wait and see," said Soutine.

He was moving, crossing the chamber to a tunnel at the other end. The mouth of the tunnel was barred with a barrier and a metal badge. Soutine pointed his flashlight at it: DÉFENSE D'ENTRER.

"We're not allowed—" started Nell. But it was too late. Soutine had already climbed over it and was disappearing into the darkness beyond.

NINETEEN

*V*ery quickly, the passage that Soutine led them along narrowed. The ceiling got lower and lower, and the only way to continue was to drop down onto all fours and crawl.

"Soutine," called Xavier from the back, "are you sure about this?"

Nell was wondering the exact same thing. The tunnel was closing in on them. She felt as if her whole body was filling the space. The roughness of the walls grazed her shoulders and hips. It was barely wide enough to move.

"Do you want to see this or not?" whispered Soutine. "Switch your flashlights off." Nell complied, tucking hers into the back pocket of her jeans. For a minute, the all-enveloping blackness tried to spark a panic, but she brushed it away. It was easier crawling without a flashlight. Very slowly, she inched her way along in the darkness, like a worm burrowing through soil. Could the tunnel get any narrower? If it did, she might get stuck, like a cork in a bottle. It wasn't a pleasant thought.

"Ouch!" Nell's head butted up against something in front of her. It was Paulette, who had stopped abruptly. Now Xavier bumped into Nell. Nell wriggled; she wanted to stretch, but there was no space. The floor of the tunnel was wet. Trickles of water ran down the walls.

"It's blocked!" Soutine called back "There's a kind of grate."

"Oh well," said Nell, cramped and uncomfortable. She wasn't sure if she would be able to turn around. They'd have to reverse. "Maybe we'd better—"

"We're not going back, if that's what you're thinking," Soutine cut in. "I can see light on the other side. And I can still smell that . . . Anyone got a screwdriver? Paul? Paulette?" He had switched his flashlight on again, and the weak light filtered back, not that Nell could see much with Paulette's behind almost filling the tunnel ahead of her.

"Nope," the twins said together.

"I've got these," said Xavier. "Reach your hand back, Nell, but be careful."

Nell reached back and Xavier put something into her hand. She felt the looped handles of Michel's scissors, the cold metal of the blades. She passed the scissors to Paulette, who passed them to Paul, who passed them to Soutine.

"Can you hear that?"

It was a low hum, the kind generated by electricity.

"We're not going back until we've seen what's going on," Soutine said again.

Nell sighed. Her knees were hurting and it was cold. What were they doing, squeezed one after the other in this tunnel? They were definitely trespassing. Up ahead, she could hear Soutine jabbing at the grate with the scissors. He exclaimed, using a word she hadn't heard before.

"He's useless at stuff like that," muttered Xavier.

"Put the point of the scissors into the head of the screw. Can you see the head of a screw?" asked Paulette with the tired air of a teacher explaining something for the billionth time.

"Of course I can," Soutine shouted angrily.

"It's round, with a little cross in it," added Paul. "Put the scissor point onto that little cross and turn." There was a short silence. Some fumbling, the sound of dropped scissors, some more fumbling and muttering.

"Got it! One down, loads more to go!"

They waited as Soutine stabbed and unscrewed. The smell of fresh bread was unmistakable, eclipsing all the other smells. Nell's tummy rumbled.

"Done," called Soutine triumphantly. One by one, they managed to twist around to slither backward through the tiny opening, dropping feetfirst into a larger tunnel below.

"This is it!" said Soutine. "Look!" He was sprawled on his stomach, his face and flashlight pressed up against the place where the wall met the floor. He drew back to reveal a sort of slot, covered in a thin wire mesh, about the size of a mailbox. There were other ones, too, a series of them at equal intervals all the way along the tunnel.

Nell flung herself down. Her chin grazed the floor, but if she kept her head as low as possible and pointed her flashlight straight at the wire mesh, she could just see through the slot. At first, she couldn't make out a thing. She was aware the others had also positioned themselves in front of the remaining slots, and the beams of their flashlights danced around, trying to pick out whatever was below.

Carefully, she tracked her flashlight one way, then the other. There were things, big, hulking things, shrouded in gloom. She found one and leveled her flashlight at it. A cluster of gigantic steel vats. Next to them were what looked like enormous bowls with monstrous-looking contraptions hovering over them, armed with hooks and claws. Nell swung her flashlight the other way. A whole wall of things that looked like . . . ovens?

"Wow, those are big machines," breathed Paulette next to her. She was doing something to the mesh with Michel's scissors, snipping away so she had a clearer view.

There were no people down there. It was deserted. The whole place, apart from a steady hum, was utterly quiet. Nell rubbed her eyes. The huge appliances made her feel like one of the Borrowers.

"Give me the camera, Paul," said Paulette.

"But it's too dark, and there's hardly any film left, and I wanted to take pictures of—"

Nell heard a scuffle. The twins were fighting over the camera.

"Stop it! Look," Soutine breathed. Something was happening. A rumbling sound was coming from the space below, and one of the walls seemed to be splitting in two. Nell was dimly aware that Paulette had won the tussle over the camera and was holding it up, finger poised over the shutter.

In the sudden flash, Nell saw that the wall wasn't actually a wall at all, and it wasn't splitting. It was a gigantic door that was swinging open, and two beams were boring bright holes of light through the dark, while the rumbling sound of engines filled the air. They were trucks! Three of them, driving down a ramp and stopping in the space below.

There was a click and a whirring noise, and then the lights flashed on, harsh white lights so bright they hurt Nell's eyes. Now she could see what lay below. A kitchen! A giant one, with industrial-size appliances and a conveyer belt linking everything up. Nell watched as several men leaped out of the trucks, shouting to one another, calling instructions. They moved out of sight, and there were clanging noises, and then they reappeared pushing tall, tiered carts.

A sharp intake of breath came from Soutine. The carts were laden with bread. The men wheeled them over to the trucks and started loading, tray upon tray of long, thin baguettes, skinny *ficelles*, crusty *pains de campagne*. Next came perfectly shaped croissants, *pains au chocolat, pains aux raisins*. And then cakes: *religieuses*, éclairs, millefeuilles, *tartes aux pommes*.

When everything was loaded and the doors slammed shut, the men leaped back into the cabs, the engines rumbled to life, and the trucks reversed out.

"Do you see what it says on the side of the trucks?" breathed Paulette.

Nell leaned forward, pressing her face up against the wire mesh so she could just see the truck nearest to her before it disappeared. In big curly orange script were the words PAIN-TASTIQUE.

They were approaching the den, chattering nonstop about what they had seen, when Neige appeared. She had released her hair from its usual tight braids, and it rippled over her shoulders, making her look as though she had stepped straight out of a Pre-Raphaelite painting.

"At last!" Her usual poise had disappeared, and she was hopping up and down as if she had been stung by a bee. Nell could see she was bursting to tell them something.

"You'll never guess what Soutine discovered!" said Paul.

"Pain-tastique—" started Paulette. But Neige cut Paulette off with a wave of her hand. She was looking at Nell with shining eyes.

"I've found something! At the doctor's office this morning."

Nell took the thing that Neige thrust at her and turned it over in her hands. It was *Paris Match*, the kind of weekly magazine—crammed with gossip and pictures of famous people—that Melinda longed to be featured in.

"Do you see?" urged Neige. "I swiped it when the receptionist wasn't looking!"

Nell looked at the photograph of the young woman on the front cover. She was standing outside a theater. Her head was thrown back and she was laughing—great peals of laughter, it looked like—exposing a long, graceful neck.

But it wasn't the woman that caught Nell's attention or the caption that ran in bold type all the way along the bottom of the cover: "From Rags to Riches: Parisian Foundling Makes It Big!"

It was the dress that Nell was staring at, a beautiful pale-green dress, exceedingly simple, except for the waterfall of ruffles running from elbow to wrist.

Nell felt something in her throat catch.

The dress was embroidered with exactly the same blue birds and cherry blossoms that adorned the precious scrap of fabric buried in her pocket—possibly with thread purchased from Marie's Mercerie.

"She's an actress, Nell," breathed Neige. "Coco Swann! Perrine must have finished the dress. And it was for her." Her eyes were huge. She was clutching Nell's arm so hard it hurt.

Nell looked at the picture again and then back at Neige.

She could almost hear an imaginary orchestra playing inside her head as her heart swelled.

"Oh!" she said, unable to find any words. Maybe she *wouldn't* have to wait until Monday for any crumbs of information that Melinda might scatter her way. Maybe she could find out where Pear was right now.

TWENTY

ell was a collector of information. She liked to do things properly, so she sat down and read the article in *Paris Match* from beginning to end in the hope that there might be some information about Pear.

There was none.

Instead, she learned that Coco Swann was a child runaway who had brought herself up on the streets of Paris, that she had been spotted singing and tap dancing by a theater impresario when she was just sixteen, and that she liked dancing at Jimmy's and drinking champagne at Café de Flore. She was currently starring in a musical comedy called *Funny Face* at the Théâtre de la Madeleine.

"Would you like me to go there with you now?" asked

Neige. "There'll be a matinee starting soon. We'll catch her before she goes on and ask her when she last saw Perrine."

They decided to split up for the afternoon. Xav, Soutine, and the twins were going to spy on the Pain-tastique stores. There was something fishy going on, something . . . secretive. "Otherwise, why would the bread factory be underground?" said Soutine. It was really peculiar, they all agreed, that so many new stores were opening while the Thing was rampaging its way through the traditional boulangeries.

Meanwhile, Nell and Neige set off for the theater via the tunnels. Nell was beginning to see how varied the underground was, almost as if it was divided into different neighborhoods. Near the den, the main tunnel was like a tree trunk, with wavy branches flying off from side to side. This morning, the passages they had slithered along had felt more like a wormery, as though something had made the tunnel by burrowing its way through the earth. Now they were back in hospitable territory: a wide, straight, sandy-floored tunnel, with no stooping required and not a squelchy area in sight.

They didn't have to go far before reaching a narrow door that led into the crypt of L'Église de la Madeleine. "Thank goodness they haven't closed this entrance yet," muttered

Neige as they tiptoed through the crypt, a place of vaults and arches, and then up some stairs into a dimly lit space full of sculptures and paintings. Outside, the light was dazzling. Corinthian columns disappeared into a bright-blue sky. It looked more like a Greek temple than a church.

After the cool of the tunnels, the heat was blistering. Nell peeled off her sweatshirt and tied it around her waist, and Neige rolled her socks down around her ankles. Then they made their way through a covered passageway and along the shady side of several narrow streets until they came to the theater, halfway along the Rue de Surène.

The man in the box office was eating his lunch. "No can do, I'm afraid," he said, setting his sandwich down. The waxed-paper wrapping, Nell noticed, was printed with the Pain-tastique logo. "The matinee starts soon. She never likes to be disturbed before a show."

"Tell her it's about Perrine Chaumet," said Neige with an authoritative air.

"She wouldn't come up if you were both the Queen of England," said the man. He eyed them beadily and, picking up his sandwich again, took a big, messy bite.

Nell tugged Neige back so they were out of sight of the man. On the other side of the lobby was a door marked STALLS. If they could pass through that, they could get to the stage. And if they could get up onstage, they could exit via the wings and go to the actors' dressing rooms.

Quickly, Nell signaled to Neige to drop down on all fours, and they half crawled, half scuttled across the lobby to the door, which banged shut as they scampered through it.

"Hey!" shouted the man. But it was too late. They were already running down the stairs, taking them two at a time, pushing through doors into the dark theater, running down to the pit, and helping each other clamber onto the stage.

The lights flashed on. "What's going on?" someone shouted.

"Nothing! Don't worry!" blustered Nell, and then they were exiting stage left and thundering along a corridor, slamming open anything that looked like a dressing-room door.

"Hey!" A woman poked her head out of a door farther down the corridor. "What's all this racket?" She was wearing a rose-patterned kimono, her hair was hidden underneath a blue turban, and her face was covered in thick white gunk.

"Coco Swann?" asked Neige breathlessly.

"It is I," said Coco Swann grandly. "How did you get past Grumpy Chops?"

"He wouldn't let us talk to you," said Nell, "and I know

it's nearly your matinee and everything, but we won't be long . . ."

Coco blew on her nails. They were long and painted the color of sunsets. Even with the white gunk covering her face, she exuded an air of film-star glamour.

"Quickly, then," she said. "You've got two minutes." She nodded at them to follow her into her dressing room.

"Excuse the face mask," she said, flopping down on a yellow chaise longue and then almost immediately springing up again, giving Neige an unexpectedly hard stare.

"I know you!" she said. "Don't you work at Crown Couture? I shouldn't be speaking with you. The way Monsieur treated—"

"Perrine?" interrupted Nell. The blood in her veins started to fizz and pop. Coco did know Pear.

Coco shifted her gaze from Neige to Nell. Against the white of the mask, her dark eyes flashed with suspicion.

"What's all this about? What do you want with Perrine?" she demanded.

"We're looking for her," said Nell, unable to contain her excitement. "We saw you wearing her dress on the cover of *Paris Match*, and we wondered if you might know where she is?"

"I can't tell you that," said Coco. She pressed her

lips firmly together and wrapped her kimono tightly around her.

"Oh, but please, you must!" cried Nell.

"Two minutes is up," said Coco. She crossed the room and pulled a red rope so a distant bell sounded. "There, Grumpy Chops will be down any minute. Off you go."

"Please don't make us go. It's just very, very important that I find Perrine," implored Nell. Why was Coco being so secretive?

"She's not in Paris," said Coco abruptly. Her gaze held Nell's, and a flicker of something—was it recognition?—registered in her eyes.

"Who *are* you? You haven't even told me your names. Don't they teach manners anymore?"

"I'm sorry. I'm Nell and this is Neige."

Coco's hand flew to her throat, the pressure of her touch releasing a puff of white powder into the air.

"Minou?" She was staring at Nell as if she had seen a ghost.

"What?" started Nell. But now Coco was distracted. Something was going on outside: doors slamming, the sound of yelled instructions, more shouting, and then heavy boots pounding along the corridor. The dressing-room door burst open, and a crowd of uniformed men crashed in.

"What on earth is this?" cried Coco.

But no one paid any attention to her. Instead, the men were surrounding Nell—crowding in on her, hemming her in, like an ugly rugby scrum, the sharp edges of their Municipal Department badges scraping at her skin and catching on her hair. All she could see was a sea of gray uniforms. She couldn't breathe. What did they want with her? Had they discovered that she had lied about her identity? That she had pretended to be Neige?

"We'll take over from here, Mademoiselle Swann."

Nell tried to scream, but a hand clamped over her mouth to silence her protests. Rough fingers lifted her up, grasping her by the armpits and dragging her outside. She could hear Coco shouting, and for a split second, she glimpsed the wide open O of Neige's mouth.

"Mademoiselle Swann, calm yourself." Nell recognized the voice, but she could not place it. "Young Magnificent here is all alone in Paris. Things have changed since your day, you know. We don't allow children to fend for themselves anymore!"

Nell was dimly aware of being bundled into a car, driven a short distance, and then being frog-marched up some steps, along a passage, and through a door. Unceremoniously, the men had pushed her into a chair, and in the intervening scuffle, her hands had been tied behind her back. Now that the men had left, she took in her surroundings. She was in a parlor full of overstuffed furniture, every surface crammed with ornaments. Opposite her, side by side, sat Cigarette Holder and Lorgnette.

"What's happening?" cried Nell angrily. "I wasn't underground! I haven't broken the law! Those Municipal Department men have got no right doing this! Untie my hands!"

"We've been following you," said Cigarette Holder, taking a long drag on her cigarette. "And haven't *you* been flitting about all over the place."

And then Nell knew. Of course it wasn't about her pretending to be Neige. It was going to be about the cursed bag.

"We'd *love* to know what you were up to in the theater," said Lorgnette, lowering the glass so Nell had the full benefit of her fish-eyed gaze.

"Wouldn't you like to know," said Nell as rudely as she could. She wondered if they had been following her the entire time she'd been here. The thought gave her the creeps.

"Now, now," said Cigarette Holder. "You must know that the rules regarding abandoned children are just the same in

France as they are in England. You need looking after. We have a duty of care."

"Where's Neige?"

"Gone home to Mother. We told her she'd best keep out of our way if she wants to hold on to her job."

"Giving you trouble, is she?" A third voice. Someone who had entered the room so quietly that no one knew he was there until he spoke.

Whoever it was stood behind Nell. She couldn't see him, but there was something about his high-pitched, almost babyish voice that made the hairs on the back of her neck stand on end.

"Monsieur Mayor! Young Magnificent, as requested."

"Excellent work, ladies, very good." The speaker was moving, walking past Nell and then slowly turning around.

Nell felt a chill seep into her bones when she saw who it was. So this was the mayor. The man who was going to such lengths to eradicate the children of Paris from the tunnels. She had seen him before and had hoped she would never set eyes on him again. He was the exact same person who had so brutally punched the waiter that first night at the hotel.

TWENTY-ONE

The mayor's raisin eyes were as hard as pebbles and full of violence. He took a step toward Nell and she recoiled.

"Where are your parents?" he asked. His voice was slippery soft and laced with menace. He didn't bother to introduce himself or explain why she had been kidnapped and tied up.

"I don't know!" said Nell. And that was the truth. She *didn't* know where they were staying. And what did the mayor want with them, anyway? They'd had drinks together at the hotel when he'd punched the waiter. They'd had lunch together the next day. It seemed they had been friends, and now they weren't.

She didn't trust any of them.

"You're lying." He started to rock slowly back and forth on his heels. He cracked his knuckles. Nell could feel the palms of her hands getting sweaty and hot.

"I'm not," she said stubbornly. She wasn't sure what was at stake, but if she told him her parents were right here in Paris, she knew she would relinquish what little control she had.

She eyed his hands, imagining one curling itself into a fist, shooting out and catching her—*BAM*—on the forehead. He had thick sausage fingers. On his middle finger, he wore a large gold ring. It was engraved with the letters *VH*.

She had seen those letters somewhere before.

"Tell me where they are, and I'll let you go." His gaze was unnerving. He didn't blink; he just stared.

Nell clamped her lips tightly shut. There was something about him that . . . simmered. As though at any moment he might explode.

"I'm waiting," he said. He was slowly curling and uncurling his fists.

"I told you: I don't know," said Nell. She wasn't going to tell him anything. Any chance she had of finding Pear would fly out the window if she did.

"Fibber," said the mayor, his eyes narrowed to slits.

"They've stolen something of mine, and I want it back. They won't get away with it."

"What have they stolen?" asked Nell. But before the question even flew out of her mouth, she knew the answer. The same *VH* that was engraved on his ring was stamped on the gobbledygook! The mayor was VH! She remembered reading the newspaper article aloud in the den: Monsieur Henri, that was his name.

"Never you mind," shot back the mayor. But she *did* mind. And now it was clear. The gobbledygook that her parents wanted so badly belonged to the mayor. And only *she* knew where it was.

"Does the name Perrine Chaumet mean anything to you?"

The question was unexpected. Nell swallowed hard. Her body went icy cold.

"I hear you've been looking for her."

"Who told you that?" asked Nell.

"I've been doing some business with your parents. And they asked me for a favor. Did you know there is a warrant out for Mademoiselle Chaumet's arrest?"

"She didn't steal the brooch!" shouted Nell. "She's not a criminal!"

"The brooch," echoed the mayor. He laughed quietly to himself. It wasn't a pleasant sound. "That's what you think this is all about, do you? Well, for your information, Mademoiselle Chaumet is currently out of the country. But when she returns, all I will have to do is snap my fingers, and it'll be jail for her."

"You're bluffing," said Nell.

"I am not."

Nell felt like something was strangling her, sucking the life out of her, and she didn't know how to stop it.

"Think about it," said the mayor. "If you can help, good. If not, let's just say it'll be bad news for Mademoiselle Chaumet and bad news for you. Madame," he turned to Lorgnette, "can you take a dictation please?"

Nell watched as Lorgnette rushed over to an ornate bureau in the corner of the room, retrieved a pad of paper and a pen, and returned to the settee, pen poised.

"Found. Penelope Magnificent, daughter of Gerald and Melinda Magnificent," dictated the mayor. *"If she remains uncollected, a week from today she will be placed in the care of the French authorities. The British authorities will be notified. Got it?"*

"Got it," said Lorgnette, setting the paper down.

"Would you like it placed in tonight's edition of *Le Monde*?" asked Cigarette Holder.

"I would, Madame."

"They won't come," interrupted Nell. "They're not bothered about me. And anyway, they can't read French."

The mayor rolled his eyes, stood up, and made for the door.

"Has anyone ever told you what a tiresome little sneak you are?"

Yes, thought Nell, *many times.*

"I'll ask you one last time," he said. "Tell me where they are, and I'll let you go. Even if it is to rush back to your vermin friends."

"No," said Nell. More than anything, she wanted to go back to Coco and find out what she had been about to say. But not like this. Something sinister was going on. The mayor was connected to the gobbledygook. The *VH* on his ring was proof of it. Her parents were embroiled in it, too, but why? She could not help this man out in any way, shape, or form. It would be a betrayal of Xavier and the rest.

"Madame, tell the newspaper to print the notice in English. And you," he swiveled his pebble-hard raisin eyes back to Nell, "shall stay here until your parents turn up to claim you. Or until you decide to protect the fate of your beloved Perrine and tell us where they are."

The mayor cracked his knuckles again. His ring winked. And he was gone.

The room they took her to was on the top floor of the house. It was suffocatingly hot with a tiny window that was too high to see out of. Nell flopped down onto the narrow bed. She examined the marks on her wrists where the rope had bound them. They were an angry red. A bracelet of welts. A sob caught in her throat. This was worse than being at Summer's End. She was a pawn caught in the middle of her parents and the mayor. She'd picked up her mother's bag because it summed up everything she detested about her parents. It had been an act of rebellion. A quick way to punish Melinda for all the years of hurt. But never in a million years did she imagine it would lead to this.

It's a good thing you didn't help the mayor, a small voice said inside her head. *How can you help someone who hates children so much?*

But you can't just stay trapped here either, another voice piped up.

He's dangerous, said the first voice. *It would be a betrayal to help him. But if you help him, you can go back to Coco. Find out what she was talking about. Find out why she called you Minou.*

Nell turned over and buried her face in the pillow. She

allowed a few tears to escape, and then she sat up and dug Pear's letter out from her pocket.

> *. . . something has happened and I need to set it right. Do not lose faith. We will be together and the truth will come out.*

Nell breathed deeply in and out, employing the panic-quelling breaths she used to fight the fear of the dark. Coco had said Pear had gone away. The mayor had said she was out of the country! Pear said she was setting something right. Was she proving a truth? Or had Nell gotten her all wrong, and she was, as Melinda said, "bad news."

Nell needed answers. She *had* to go back to Coco. But, no way was she going to help the mayor. She would get out of here on her own.

Much later, when the room was beginning to cool and the light outside had dimmed, Cigarette Holder and Lorgnette unlocked the door and marched Nell back downstairs.

In the kitchen, a table was set for three, and a pungent aroma filled the air.

"We've been cooking," announced Cigarette Holder. "Rabbit stew."

The stew was not the worst Nell had tasted, but she was not hungry. Nevertheless, she persevered, gingerly chewing each mouthful about a million times before swallowing. If she was going to escape, she needed to be strong, so she forced down as many morsels as she could.

Eventually, the plates were cleared and Nell was marched out of the kitchen and back to the overstuffed parlor. In the hall, the front door beckoned. Nell's whole body tingled. Could she simply make a dash for it? It was about three long strides.

"Don't even try it," said Cigarette Holder, clamping her hand down on Nell's shoulder. "The doors and windows are all triple locked. You wouldn't stand a chance."

In the parlor, they sat her down between them on the overstuffed sofa. They wanted to play games.

"Hangman? Tic-tac-toe? Battleship?"

Lorgnette passed around pencils and paper. The piece of paper she gave to Nell was blank on one side, and on the other . . . a page of curls and loops and circles.

Nell plucked it up and stared.

It looked exactly like the page of gobbledygook she had found in her mother's bag.

"What's this?" she asked, holding it up.

"Don't tell me that you've never seen shorthand

before?" sneered Lorgnette. "Agnes, she doesn't know about shorthand."

"We always take dictation in shorthand," said Cigarette Holder. "It's how we were taught years ago at the Duployan Secretarial School."

Nell looked at the loops and swirls, the dots and circles. There in the corner was the stamp, a tiny circle with *VH* on the inside, just the same as on the page of gobbledygook. But there was something else, too. Some sort of design had been impressed onto the paper. She glanced at the two women. They were busy drawing dots in preparation for a game of Battleship. Surreptitiously, she held the paper up to the light. There it was. A watermark. Like the Basildon Bond one on the writing paper she kept in her desk drawer at home. Except this didn't say Basildon Bond.

It said . . . Pain-tastique.

TWENTY-TWO

That night, locked in the airless room at the top of the house, Nell could not sleep. It wasn't just because it was pitch-black or felt hard to breathe, although obviously neither of those things helped. It was her thoughts that disturbed her, running riot around and around in her head, stabbing this way and that. What did the mayor have to do with Pain-tastique? Why was he so desperate to get his hands on the gobbledygook? And could he really threaten to arrest Pear?

Nell tried to marshal her thoughts, to line them up in order. Tomorrow was Sunday. Just one day before she was due to meet her parents at Gare du Nord. She had to escape. But how could she do that? Even in sleep, her brain kept whirring, her dreams a muddle of Pear, the mayor, and her parents, an endless maze of underground tunnels, pages and pages of gobbledygook and plastic dishes stamped with s13.

After the longest time, when the blackness had receded and a dim light crept in from the high window, the door was unlocked and she was taken down for breakfast. They had barely sat down at the kitchen table when the doorbell rang.

"Who can that be at this early hour?" said Cigarette Holder. And then, "Stop!" because Nell had already shoved her chair back and was thundering out of the kitchen and down the passageway to the front door.

"Let me out!" she yelled, so loud her lungs hurt. She pummeled the door with such force she could feel the skin splitting, her knuckles screaming with pain. Whoever was on the other side must hear her!

But it was no good. One of the women caught hold of her and dragged her back into the kitchen.

"Do I have to tie you up again, you wretch?" Lorgnette hissed. "Sit down this instant! As soon as you've had breakfast, you are going straight back to your room!"

Nell sat. How was she ever going to escape? They were like hawks. And they were so strong. It was going to be impossible.

The kitchen door opened again and Cigarette Holder

stumped in. She was carrying a white cardboard cake box that she set triumphantly down on the table.

"Look! We have fresh pastries! A delightful little Tunisian boy delivered them: said he'd been sent by Pain-tastique. And you know what that means. Victor's thinking of us." She looked at Nell, who was looking at the pastry box. "Don't think you're getting one," she snapped.

Nell sat very still, allowing Cigarette Holder's words to sink in. A Tunisian boy! Could it be Soutine? Or was that too much of a coincidence? Maybe—her heart lifted a little as she grasped at a sliver of hope—there was a message for her in the box.

Lorgnette grabbed the box and opened it to reveal two plump almond croissants. She looked at Nell with mock concern. "I'm afraid you'll just have to do with bread and a bit of jam."

"Fine," said Nell, breaking off the end of the baguette that was handed to her. She watched as the pair bit into their croissants, scattering crumbs of flaky pastry everywhere. Reaching for the jam, she nudged the cake box closer to her. Looked inside. It was empty apart from a few crumbs. No note, then. Accidentally on purpose she knocked the box off the table and onto the floor.

"Watch it!"

"Sorry," said Nell, scrabbling to pick it up. Nothing. There was no message or clue on the front, back, or sides of the box at all. Of course it hadn't been Soutine. There was more than one Tunisian boy in Paris!

"That was diiiivine," drawled Cigarette Holder.

"Deeeliiiicious," agreed Lorgnette.

Very briefly, Lorgnette's eyes rolled back in their sockets. She slapped her own cheek as if to wake herself up. Shakily, she poured herself a coffee. Slurped it down.

"Giiiive meeee sooome of thaaat," said Cigarette Holder. She could barely speak. Nell watched, fascinated. Their heads were lolling. Their hands clawed at the table, desperately trying to keep their bodies upright.

Smash. The coffee cup that Lorgnette was wavering in the direction of her lips crashed to the floor, splintering into a thousand tiny pieces.

Bam. Cigarette Holder's head thudded down onto the table and stayed there.

Thump. Lorgnette sagged to one side and then slumped down in her chair, chin to chest.

Nell stared.

Whether they were asleep or dead, this was her chance.

Quickly, she pushed back her chair. Prodded Cigarette Holder. No response. Prodded Lorgnette. A guttural snore. She had to find the keys and get out now. As fast as she could, she ran back to the front door. Frantically, she scanned the surrounding hall for signs: cupboards, hooks, safes, anywhere keys would be kept. Nothing. Back into the kitchen. Where to start? Hands in Cigarette Holder's pockets (a cigarette stub, a peppermint), then Lorgnette's pockets (one franc, a Métro ticket). No keys. Back into the hall. Tugging at the door. Kicking at it. Shouting with frustration. Cigarette Holder had opened the door to accept the pastries. Where was the key?

Back into the kitchen, pulling out drawers, yanking open cupboards. *Be methodical,* she told herself. *Slow down.* She approached Cigarette Holder. The key hadn't been in her pocket. *Might it be . . . ?* She felt around the woman's neck for a chain. She had a scrawny neck, and Nell could feel a tendon pulsating, but there was no chain, no key. She dug her hands under the woman's sweater, felt around her waist. *Yes!* A belt. And dangling from it, keys. Three of them.

Back to the front door. First key in the lock. It didn't fit. *Try another! No. Try the third one. No!* A scream of frustration. Again, Nell tried to jam them in. Again and again. Her hands were shaking. They wouldn't turn!

Back into the kitchen. Her captors were still immobile.

Something twitched rhythmically in the pouchy bit beneath Lorgnette's left eye.

Think, think. What would the others do? She raked her fingers through her hair, tearing at the knots.

Of course! She was being stupid. *They'd go downstairs, not up! The cellar!* Back into the hall. Through the door at the end. And yes, steps leading down to a basement. *Oh, please,* thought Nell. *Please let there be a way into the tunnels.*

It was a cobwebby place, packed with junk.

Nell pushed a crate crammed with things wrapped in newspaper over to the side of the room. She couldn't even see the floor, there was so much stuff! She dragged another crate over, heaved up boxes, and set them down. Something clattered to the floor. She stooped to pick it up. It was a lamp attached to a leather belt. No, the strap was too short for a belt. Nell turned the switch on at the base of the lamp. A steady white beam illuminated the room. It was a headlamp! Quickly, she strapped it to her forehead, buckling it up at the back. She turned in a circle, the light swooping around with her. If there was a flashlight down here, surely that might mean access to the tunnels? Frantically, she carried on clearing the floor. She worked as quickly as she could, listening for a tread on the stair just in case the two women woke up. And then she shoved a small trunk out of the way and saw . . .

A trap door. Padlocked.

Nell sat back on her haunches. Breathed out. Breathed in. Breathed out again. Slowly, purposefully, she extracted the keys from her pocket. Tried again. And somehow, even before she slid the second key in the lock, she just knew it was going to work. *Yes!* It turned smoothly, and then with a satisfying click, the padlock sprang open. Freedom at last. Adjusting the headlamp so the flashlight part sat squarely in the middle of her forehead, she began her descent.

TWENTY-THREE

She had expected a ladder, like the one below the Crillon. But instead, she found herself making her way down a spiral staircase that seemed to go on forever: ten, twenty, fifty steps. Then there was a ladder. That went on and on, too. She felt like she was descending to the very center of the earth.

Finally, when she reached the bottom, there were no comforting flashlights stuck into jam jars waiting for her. It didn't matter. She had the headlamp, and it shone reassuringly, throwing a steady beam of light in whichever direction she turned.

The trouble was, with no bearings, she didn't know which way to go.

She thought back to yesterday, walking with Neige

though the tunnels to L'Église de la Madeleine. It hadn't been far from the den. But then at the theater, she'd been bundled into the car and too panicked to see where they were going. How long had they driven for? A picture of the Seine River popped into her head, a silvery ribbon cutting through the center of Paris. Had they driven over a bridge, or was she imagining it? Perhaps they had crossed from the Right Bank to the Left. The Left Bank was where the students, the writers, the artists and philosophers lived. It was where the universities were—and the jazz clubs. Oh! Had they crossed the river? She didn't know!

Here she was, with tunnels stretching away in all directions, straggling off this way and that, in a subterraneous maze.

"Ip dip, sky blue, who's it? Not you," she muttered under her breath, nodding from one passageway to another. There were four of them in total, all disappearing into the great unknown. The rhyme landed on the passage closest to her, so she started to follow that one. It might not lead to the den, but it would eventually lead to another exit.

After what seemed like a very long time, she came to another crossroads. A narrow passage to her right seemed to swing upward. Up must be good. She trudged along, swinging her head from side to side for optimum illumination. And then, without any fanfare, there it was. A flight of steps cut into the stone wall. Relief flooded her. A loud laugh shot out of her mouth.

The stairs went on for ages. In some places, they had all but crumbled away and she had to clutch at the wall, feeling for jaggedy bits to cling on to. But at last she was at the top and . . . a great rush of despair engulfed her. It was blocked. A sheet of metal nailed down with giant bolts. She kicked at it fruitlessly. Even Paul and Paulette with their screwdrivers and bolt cutters could not have broken into this.

Back she went, down the stairs, which seemed to be even more precarious now that there wasn't the promise of escape at the end. And when she reached the bottom, she couldn't remember which direction she'd come from. A sob borne out of frustration rather than fear lurched its way out of her throat.

Doggedly, she "ip dipped" and took the passageway straight ahead. It wriggled its way up and down, but there were no more ladders, or stairs, or anything resembling bids for freedom. She could hear dripping. Everything was wet. The walls and ceilings seemed to be oozing water. She was ankle-deep in mud.

There were hundreds and hundreds of miles of tunnels below Paris. Two hundred, Xavier had said. What if she walked and walked and couldn't find an exit, ever? It was like being lost in a maze. She had no food and no drink. She might tramp around and around in circles, getting weaker and weaker by the minute, and then collapse and die.

Pull yourself together, Nell, be rational, she told herself. But then she turned a corner and nothing, *nothing* could have prepared her for what she saw next.

She screamed.

She was staring at the most macabre scene she had ever seen in her life. Lining the walls were bones, millions of them, packing the wall in spine-tingling patterns: stacks of tibias, femurs, and . . . no! Was that really . . . ? Nell clamped her eyes shut in horror and then tentatively opened them again. There were actual skulls! Thousands of them, their empty eye sockets boring into her, manic grinning mouths leering at her.

Nell stumbled back. The black eye holes followed her. Her scream turned to a whimper, like a dog frightened out of its wits. What was this place? Were these the bones of people like her who'd gotten lost and never escaped?

Nell turned and ran, the beam of the headlamp jerking up and down, bouncing crazily this way and that. On she ran, panting and stumbling, twisting and turning, blind to where she was going but desperate to get away.

But the bones wouldn't leave her. In her imagination, they were scrambling after her—legs, arms, spines, skulls forming whole skeletons in her head, dancing, prancing, rattling, jangling . . . *Thud.* She had slammed into something solid, something large, something . . . human?

For a second, the only thing she could hear was the raggedy sound of her breathing and her heart beating like a drum in her ears. She stared at the floor, too scared to look up. And then strong arms were reaching out, a gentle hand steadying her.

"Are you OK, little one?" A man's voice. She *thought* it sounded kind. "Are you OK?"

Fearfully, she forced her eyes to swivel sideways. No bones, just a rough-hewn stone wall.

She dared to slide her eyes back to the front. A man with floppy brown hair was looking at her with concern.

"Papa! She's crying."

Behind him, craning to see her, was a small child.

TWENTY-FOUR

There are skeletons," she said. Her voice was shaking.

"Papa! She went to the catacombs. We were just going there." The child was holding a flashlight shaped like a mouse. She waved it around excitedly as she talked. It had pink illuminated ears and a little tail.

"What are you talking about?" Confused, Nell looked from the child to the man called Papa.

"You don't know about the catacombs?" said the child. "It's where they keep the bones!"

"What? Why? You were *going* there?"

She looked at the man again, horrified. "You can't take a little girl there!"

"Mimi, shh." The man hushed the child. He turned back

to Nell and bent down so his eyes were level with hers. "Are you lost?"

"Yes."

"Well, then, you must come with us. We will show you the way out. Mimi, we'll have to postpone our outing until tomorrow."

He turned and strode away.

"*Now* Gil will wish he'd come, instead of playing marbles," said the little girl happily. "Wait till he sees what we've found! Come on, we'll look after you." She was only about six, but she had a maternal air about her. She grabbed Nell's hand and bustled along after the man, wiggling her mouse flashlight this way and that. "The catacombs are nothing to be scared of," she said. Her tiny hand was warm and comforting.

Mimi and Gil. The names sounded familiar. Where had she heard them before?

And then she remembered. They were the children Xavier had taken the buns for on that first day. The family that lived in the tunnels after the Thing attacked their boulangerie. The Bernards!

"Once upon a time," the little girl was saying, "the graveyards in Paris were full to overflowing. They were smelly and dirty, and there was no space left to bury anybody else at all. But then the king had a brain wave. He knew there was oodles of space below the city, so he ordered that all the bones be moved from the graveyards to the tunnels."

Up ahead, Papa had stopped and was waiting for them to catch up.

"Is that true?" Nell asked him. She thought back to what she had seen. The bones had been neatly stacked in swirls and whirls, almost making patterns on the walls. She could see that people might think it looked sort of pretty until they found out what it was.

"Yes, all true," he said. "The remains of six or seven million Parisians are buried down here. We like to explore them, don't we, Mimi?"

"They moved the bones in the night," said Mimi gleefully, "in covered wagons, so people wouldn't be scared. It took twelve years, didn't it, Papa? Oh, look, we're home. Gil! *Maman*, look what we found!"

They were standing on the threshold of what looked like Aladdin's cave. A richly patterned rug covered most of the floor, and curtains draped the walls. Almost every inch was crammed with furniture: a pair of armchairs, a dresser, a chest of drawers, a kitchen table, a large mattress heaped with blankets. And that wasn't even counting all the other stuff. There were battered old suitcases and wicker baskets and paper bags bursting with clothes and cushions and other bits and bobs. It looked like an entire home had been crammed into this one cave.

Sitting on the rug, a woman was cutting an apple into quarters and passing them to a boy who was even smaller than Mimi. "Patrick! Mimi!" she said as they appeared. "And who is this?"

Patrick looked like a giant in the cave. He couldn't even stand up straight; he had to stoop his shoulders and tilt his head.

"This is . . ." He looked questioningly at Nell.

"Nell," she offered.

"She's had a scare in the catacombs."

"You poor thing!" exclaimed the woman. "I'm Pascale. Come, come." She piled a couple of bags on top of each other, making space for Nell to sit. "I'll make some tea. I don't know why they're always going off down there," she added conspiratorially. "It's not for us, is it, Gil?"

The little boy, who had been regarding Nell with suspicion, shook his head in agreement and crunched into his apple.

"Would you like a sandwich?" Pascale was already reaching for a large tin and taking paper packages out. Nell nodded. She was starving. She watched while Pascale tore off the end of a baguette and stuffed it with slabs of yellow cheese.

In the corner, Mimi was fussing over what looked like a makeshift cradle fashioned from an old wooden fruit box. Carefully, she laid her mouse flashlight in it and tucked it up in a blanket. "Night night, Minnie Minou."

Just at that moment, Pascale offered Nell her tea. Nell blew on it and took a sip. It was scalding hot and had a bitter taste. She made a face, and Pascale said, "You haven't had chamomile before?"

"No," she replied, tentatively raising the cup to her lips again.

"Try to drink it," said Pascale, handing her the sandwich. "It's calming—good after a shock."

The second sip wasn't as bad as the first.

While Nell ate, Pascale and Patrick moved around the cave talking softly to each other, sorting things in boxes while Mimi and Gil sat and stared at her.

"I'm a friend of Xavier's," she said. "He told me about you."

"Xavier!" said Mimi. "He brings us food sometimes, doesn't he, Gil?"

Pascale stopped what she was doing and came over. "We're only down here until we get back on our feet," she said quickly.

"I know what happened to you, and I might be able to help," said Nell. She wasn't entirely certain *how* she would help. But it was something to do with Pain-tastique, the mayor, and the gobbledygook. If she could just find out what it meant, she would know what to do.

The Bernards looked at her rather doubtfully, and she didn't blame them. Her jeans were torn. Her hair was even more tangled than usual. Her face was probably smeared with dirty tears. How could a small girl from England, who couldn't even navigate her way underground and was frightened of old bones, be able to stop the Thing that had ruined them?

"Will you show me the way out now?" Nell asked. It didn't matter if Patrick and Pascale thought she was talking nonsense. The mayor's face loomed large in her imagination, leering and smiling, a grotesque caricature. Whatever he was up to, she was going to stop him. And her friends would help her.

TWENTY-FIVE

The Bernards' cave was at the base of a ramp that led up to a garage door. On the other side was an underground parking garage. Patrick and Mimi led the way up a flight of stairs, through another door, and into a long corridor. Now they were aboveground. Tall windows looked out onto a quadrangle. A nervous shiver skittered up and down Nell's spine. It smelled like Summer's End—chalk dust and wax polish on the parquet flooring.

"This is where Pascale teaches," explained Patrick. "No one's here at the moment. The new semester starts in a few weeks' time."

Out on the street, Nell blinked. Everything was so bright and loud. Traffic whizzed past. A market was in full swing. The terraces of the cafés were packed with people clinking glasses and enjoying an early lunch. It seemed odd to Nell that everything was carrying on as normal. But of course it was. Time always went marching on.

The Métro station was called Montparnasse. So they were on the Left Bank. "I know where I am now," said Nell, picturing the Métro map in her head. Montparnasse was on Line Twelve, the black line that cut across Paris from north to south. She could almost sense her inner compass resetting, her pattern of Paris reassembling, everything slotting into place. It was only a few stops from here to Concorde and the den.

She was just about to say goodbye when she stopped, dimly aware that something had been flickering in the nethermost reaches of her mind. What was it? A thought that needed explaining. A fact that had been missing. And then she remembered. "Mimi, why do you call your mouse flashlight Minnie Minou?"

The question took Mimi by surprise. "Because of the cradle," she said. "It was in the cave when we arrived. The name Minou is scratched into it in tiny letters."

Nell didn't know what she would have done if the others hadn't been in the den, so it was with the most enormous sense of relief that she heard their voices.

"I'm back!" she shouted as she burst into the little cavern

and then had to battle tears as she watched their faces break into delighted grins, and they all leaped up and enveloped her in a great hug.

"It worked!" said Soutine.

"What worked?" she asked, confused.

"The sleeping potion," said Paulette.

"Soutine sprinkled it in when he was making the croissants," said Paul.

"It's his grandma's recipe, top secret, all made from herbs," added Neige.

"And they won't wake up until tomorrow morning," smiled Xavier. "They'll be out for the count for at least twenty-four hours, right, Soutine?"

"Right," said Soutine proudly.

"Oh, Soutine!" said Nell. And they smiled at each other, a proper smile. Up until now, she hadn't been sure Soutine had trusted her or even liked her. Of the five children, he had been the least welcoming. But he had done this. Entirely for her. "But how did you know where I was?"

"I followed you, of course!" said Neige. "Did you think I'd just stand by and watch you get kidnapped right under my very nose? I jumped in a taxi. I've always wanted to say *Follow that car!* like in a detective movie. And I did! Tailed you all the way over to Corvisart."

A warm feeling spread through Nell's entire body.

This is what it felt like to have proper friends.

"And you even found your way back here," said Xav with real admiration. "I told them you've got a map inside your head!"

"But why did they take you?" asked Soutine. "The ladies and the Municipal Department men. What do they want?"

"It's something to do with the mayor!" she said. "He's desperate to know where my parents are. And you know the gobbledygook? With the *VH* stamped on it? Well, he is VH!" And she told them about his ring.

Paul was sent to retrieve Melinda's bag from its hiding place. It had lost some of its former shine, the diamond clasp and gold chain having become dulled by cave dust.

Quickly, Nell dug out the paper. She passed it to Xavier.

"Hold it up to the light," she instructed.

"Why?" he said.

"Just try," insisted Nell.

Xavier held the paper against one of the light bulbs that were strung across the ceiling of the cave, but the light was too weak. Nell unstrapped her headlamp and flicked on the switch. Xav held the paper against the beam.

"What can you see?" demanded Nell.

"A sort of pattern in the paper," said Xavier slowly.

"It's called a watermark," said Nell. "Can you read it?"

"It says . . . Pain-tastique. But . . . ?" said Xav.

"So the mayor"—Neige took the paper from Xavier. Her finger hovered over the tiny *VH* stamp—"has something to do with Pain-tastique?"

"Yes!" said Nell. "I watched Cigarette Holder take dictation from the mayor yesterday. She didn't use proper writing. It was all squiggles and wriggles, just like this. I asked what it was, and she said shorthand. She learned it at some place called the Duployan School. I bet this is her writing, too."

"So all we have to do," said Xav, "is find someone who knows shorthand, someone who can translate this gobbledygook, and then we'll understand what the mayor is up to and where *this* fits in?" He was holding the small plastic S13 dish in the palm of his hand.

"*And* why my parents stole it," said Nell. She looked at them. "And there's something else. It's to do with Pear." She told them what the mayor had said.

"A warrant! So she *is* on the run!" said Soutine.

"Maybe," she said. It sounded exciting, but it really wasn't. Someone who was on the run could end up in jail.

"Don't worry, Nell," said Xav. "If we can work out what

trouble the mayor and your parents are mixed up in, maybe *that's* how we make them talk about Pear."

"We need to find someone who understands shorthand," said Paulette.

"Like a secretary? Or a reporter?" added Paul.

Something pinged in Nell's head. She grabbed the gobbledygook and the plastic dish and stuffed them back into Melinda's bag. "We need to go to Belleville right away and find Emil."

The newspaper's headquarters were at 5 Rue des Italiens, LE MONDE emblazoned across the front of the building in letters a yard high.

"What can I do for you?" asked the doorman as they all trooped in. His pompadour was as good as Elvis Presley's, and his mustache curled up in a smile.

"We've come to see Colette," said Emil, as though he strolled into newspaper offices every day. "She's my sis. She works in the newsroom on the fourth floor."

The doorman hesitated. Children didn't normally make a habit of turning up unannounced at such an important newspaper. Sometimes the senior editors came in with their families to give them "the tour." Their children would be dressed up in their Sunday best, not like this ragtag lot.

But . . . Elvis smoothed his pompadour, twiddled his mustache. It was quiet. It was the weekend. And he could see right away that this skinny kid in the green cap resembled the nervous girl who had started last week.

"Well, it is a Sunday," he said. "The big boss isn't in, and what the eye doesn't see, the heart doesn't grieve over." He picked up the phone. "Off you go. I'll call and tell her you're on your way."

The elevator deposited them in a vast room filled with typewriters and telephones. At the far end, they could hear a steady *click-clack* as someone bashed away at a typewriter. Colette rushed over to greet them. She was all jitters and nerves.

"Emil! What are you doing here?" she asked anxiously. "Did I forget something? I've got my lunch. I remembered to feed the cat. Are you locked out? I'll get the key."

"I'm not locked out or anything," said Emil. "We're here 'cause this group needs your help."

Colette glanced around, as though expecting someone to bark at her at any moment. But there were only two or three other people in the room, and their heads were down. "What do you mean they want my help?"

"Remember Nell? You met her in Perrine's apartment?"

Colette's eyes met Nell's. "Oh! It's about your friend." She turned back to Emil. "You only asked me to start digging around this morning! I haven't had a chance yet!"

"It doesn't matter," said Nell hurriedly. She wished Colette wouldn't look so anxious. It was making her feel nervous, too. She pulled the gobbledygook out of Melinda's bag and handed it over.

"Emil says you understand shorthand. Can you tell us what this means?"

Colette scanned the loops and swirls, her lips moving silently as she read. A sudden intake of breath. A gasp. "Where did you get this?" she asked, turning to them, her eyes wide.

"Why? What does it say?"

Colette was gripping the paper so hard her knuckles had gone white. Her gaze, which had been so unsure before, was now razor-sharp. She stabbed a finger at the top of the page. "It says *Terms and usage for the culture and propagation of Spore Thirteen.*"

The children stared at her, trying to make sense of the words.

S13. The small plastic dish! Something had told Nell not to open it. Now, all of a sudden, she knew why. She could picture the older girls at school dressed in white lab coats doing interesting-looking experiments. She'd wanted to join in, but the science teacher had said she'd have to wait until she was in the senior school.

It was a petri dish. For growing bacteria in.

"Don't they call the Thing that is destroying the boulangeries a spore?" Nell said. She remembered watching the news that first night.

"Bacteria form spores . . ." said Neige. "So someone has actually grown this stuff on purpose!"

"Yes!" said Colette, still scanning the gobbledygook. "These are instructions. Look what it says here—*How to grow the bacteria and what it can infect*. The list is endless: bread and groceries and wine . . ."

"So it's the mayor who's behind it all!" said Soutine in utter disgust. "Poisoning the boulangeries and opening up his own stores instead!"

And then Nell remembered. She'd been standing at the dining room door while her parents muttered about Magnificent Foods. They'd been discussing falling profits. They were worried about the board and the stipulations. Melinda had said they had to find a solution. And the solution wasn't "buy one, get one free."

What had been her exact words? Nell screwed her eyes up tight. That was it! Melinda had said they had to kill the competition.

A cold stone plopped down into the very depths of her stomach.

Could it be that her parents were going to take this S13 and use it in England? And just as the Thing had wreaked havoc in the boulangeries across Paris, it would do the very same to every grocery store at home!

eige was on her feet, twirling her braids as though they were a pair of lassos. "This is your chance, Colette! You can investigate the whole thing, write the story up. Blow everyone's cover."

"Shazam!" said Xav, and Paul and Paulette cheered.

"But . . . the editor isn't here. I'd need approval first." Colette seemed to shrink in the face of their enthusiasm. The anxious look had crept back into her eyes.

"Stuff the editor!" scoffed Soutine. "Just do it!"

"But . . ." Colette chewed on the end of her pencil.

"Colette, come on!" Paulette implored.

"What's that thing you're always going on about?" demanded Emil. "Where everyone wants to be the first to break the news?"

"A scoop," said Colette.

"It'd be the scoop of the century!" said Neige.

"The scoop to end all scoops," agreed Xav.

"Do you think I could?" Colette sat up a little straighter. She stopped chewing on her pencil and made a few tentative scribbles in her notepad.

"This is *Le Monde*," said Neige. She swept her arm out, taking in the banks of typewriters and telephones. "We can tell the story to all of France! Maybe the whole world! Oh, Colette, you can do that, can't you?"

"If the editor found out you *didn't* do it, that you let this story slip through your fingers, then you'd be in trouble," added Soutine.

Colette, who had started scribbling frantically, stopped and looked up. Her uncertain expression had vanished, and something determined gleamed in her eyes. "Yes, you are right. I *can* do it. I have to do it," she said. "And"—she tapped the gobbledygook decisively with her pencil—"we've got this as solid evidence!"

"And I've got pictures," said Paulette, "of the Pain-tastique factory."

And then everyone started chattering at once, suggestions coming thick and fast. Colette must talk to Emil about being tricked into smashing up the Concorde den. And to the Bernards about being made homeless. And to the Ben Amors about what it felt like when the Thing struck.

No one noticed how quiet Nell was. That she hadn't said a word. The truth was, her head was spinning. It *was* a good idea. But Melinda and Gerald were preparing to leave France tomorrow. They were expecting to meet her at Gare du Nord at ten o'clock. And the mayor was waiting, too. If she didn't give him Melinda and Gerald's whereabouts, he was going to arrest Pear.

Getting Colette to write the story was a brilliant idea. But it wasn't enough.

If she could somehow get the bag and the mayor and her parents in the same place at the same time, perhaps she could stop them, stop the Thing, *and* save Pear.

She would have to go back to the house in Corvisart. She could lead the mayor to her parents. Her parents would be waiting for her—and the world would be watching. If the mayor was apprehended, the threat of the warrant might be lifted, and Pear, wherever she was, could come back home.

"I've got an idea," she burst out, making everyone jump. "Yes, Colette must do the scoop, but we all have to work together. Emil, can you rally the Belleville lot? Soutine, will you tell your family and the Bernards we need their help? Colette, can you make a copy of this gobbledygook? And Neige, it's finally time to go to the police."

They were looking at her and nodding in agreement, and for a brief moment, she experienced a wonderful sense of control.

"Tell *everyone* they must be at Gare du Nord at ten tomorrow. Get all the children in Paris down there if you can. *And* every baker, whether they are still in business or not. Together we'll catch them all red-handed. *That* will be the scoop. And you," she turned to Colette, "will be there to cover it."

In the fading sunlight, the tips of Xavier's hair blazed red like sparks of fire. Everyone else had gone home. Xav said he would accompany Nell back to Corvisart, but she didn't want to go yet.

"I've got to go to the theater, Xav," she said, "to find Coco Swann. Ask her why Pear has left the country. And something else—she called me Minou. Why would she do that?"

As they hurried through the dusky streets to the theater, Nell felt the faint stirrings of hope. She imagined Coco smiling with relief when she saw her. Her eyes would light up, and she would tell Nell something important, something about Pear, something that would finally make sense.

But when they turned onto the little street, Nell's heart plummeted. The lights were off, the shutters down, the door to the theater firmly shut.

"Oh no!" she wailed. She had no idea where Coco lived. And there was no one to ask.

"'Cause it's Sunday, I expect," said Xav. "We'll come back tomorrow."

Nell tried to nod, but there was a coal-size lump in her throat. Didn't Xav realize tomorrow might be too late? She knew that if her plan didn't work, she wouldn't be able to come back. She would be on the return train to London and the dreaded Summer's End, not to mention an unhappily ever after with Melinda and Gerald.

"You hungry?" asked Xav, rattling his pockets. "I've got loads of tips. Let's go to Chartier. It's where Grandpa and I go for our birthdays. That'll cheer you up."

But even though the restaurant was charming, all high ceilings and glowing lamps, Nell's anxiety lingered. Even though they sat in the upstairs gallery, the perfect place to observe the frenetic activity below, and even though Xav ordered shrimp in Marie Rose sauce, followed by steak and *frites* and then a giant *chocolat Liégeois* crammed with ice cream, whipped cream, and rich chocolate sauce, a gnawing feeling remained in the pit of Nell's stomach.

Under the table, she crossed both fingers. Please, please let everything go according to plan tomorrow. Please, please don't let anything go wrong.

Much later, Nell followed Xav along a tangle of cobbled streets, through a hole in a brick wall to a tiny patch of shrubbery. The street lamp cast a luminous glow on the straggly grass, picking out the secret gleam of a manhole. Like thieves in the night, they slipped underground and, following Xav's spidery diagram, finally came to the ladder and steps leading up to the cellar. Just as they had expected, two dark figures were still slumped at the kitchen table, wheezing noisily. Silently, Nell and Xav crept past them and made their way up the stairs to the attic.

Nell dug in her pocket and passed Xav the keys she had taken from Cigarette Holder the day before. She was acutely aware that, if things didn't go right, she might never see or speak to him again. "Lock me in and then put these back on her belt," she said, her voice low.

"All right," he whispered. For a minute, they stood

together in the quietness of the house. They were a good team, Nell thought. She reached out and squeezed Xav's arm gratefully. "Good luck, then," said Xav softly. "See you tomorrow." A brief hug. A moment of warmth. And then he was gone, the key was turning in the lock, and Nell was all alone.

TWENTY-SEVEN

The next morning, Nell woke with a start. A square
of cerulean-blue sky blazed high above the window.
A slant of sun cut across the room. *Ouch!* Something was
digging into her stomach, pushing against her ribs. And
then she remembered. Under her sweatshirt was Melinda's
bag, its chain wrapped around her waist.

A cold fist squeezed her insides. This was it. Today was
the day. She was going to tell the mayor where her parents
were. She was going to lead him to them at Gare du Nord.
Soutine, the twins, Xav, Neige, Colette, the Belleville group,
the Bernards, and the Ben Amors were all counting on
her. She had promised them a scoop. *Please let it work!*
she thought.

Gingerly, she got out of bed and examined the

indentations on her stomach where the bag had made its mark in the night. Then she tugged her sweatshirt back down and banged on the door.

Within seconds, the key turned in the lock and the cloying smell of peppermints mixed with cigarette smoke filled the air. Cigarette Holder and Lorgnette stood on the threshold regarding her balefully. They both looked terrible, startlingly pale with raw red eyes.

"I'm ready to see the mayor," Nell blurted out.

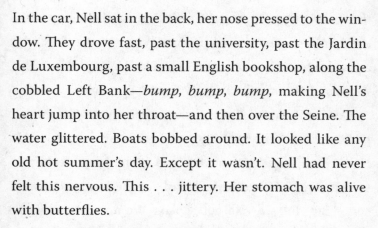

In the car, Nell sat in the back, her nose pressed to the window. They drove fast, past the university, past the Jardin de Luxembourg, past a small English bookshop, along the cobbled Left Bank—*bump, bump, bump*, making Nell's heart jump into her throat—and then over the Seine. The water glittered. Boats bobbed around. It looked like any old hot summer's day. Except it wasn't. Nell had never felt this nervous. This . . . jittery. Her stomach was alive with butterflies.

City Hall was like a grand Italian palazzo, all turrets and towers. For one fleeting moment, an image flashed through Nell's mind, of Pear locked up like Rapunzel in the top tower. She felt a sharp little pain in her chest and shook her head to dislodge the thought. This wasn't a fairy tale. This was real. The mayor was bad. He was doing bad things to real people. And her parents were going to do the same.

A couple of stern-faced Municipal Department men ushered the trio out of the car, up the steps, and into a grand entrance hall. It was huge and echoey. Nell's chest tightened. At the far end of the hall, she could see the mayor surrounded by a cluster of people bearing cameras and microphones.

A lady with a clipboard hurried across the hall toward them, her fingers to her lips. "We're just finishing up with the Pain-tastique press conference," she whispered. "Only a couple more questions, and Monsieur Henri will be right with you."

"As I was saying," said the mayor in his awful, high-pitched voice, "this boulangerie business is very, *very* sad." Nell would have laughed out loud if she hadn't been so scared. She had never, ever, heard anyone sound so insincere. "But, folks, we've got a plan. We are streamlining for the future, bringing everything under one roof. And we are *so* excited that these marvelous new Pain-tastique stores are being rolled out using the latest in health and safety measures."

"Mr. Mayor, are you saying that the boulangeries

attacked by the Thing *weren't* using the correct procedures?" asked someone, sticking a microphone under the mayor's nose.

"Unfortunately"—the mayor paused and gave a long, theatrical sigh—"the bakers have only themselves to blame. If they had taken care of their stores properly, if they had been more aware of hygiene, they wouldn't have gotten themselves into this mess in the first place."

Nell burned with indignation. How dare he blame the bakers for this Thing that HE had created? She wanted to run over there now and tell everyone, shout it from the rooftops. But she couldn't. She must stick to the plan.

"And what of the wine sellers?" a young woman called from the back of the group. "There are rumors that batches of wine are being infected, too."

Wine? Nell remembered the gobbledygook—Colette had read out a list: bread, groceries, wine. So that was next.

"We're talking about bread today," said the mayor, his raisin eyes hardening. He turned and focused his attention on the people at the front of the group. "Everyone in Paris eats bread. A baguette with each meal—breakfast, lunch, and dinner. You can rely on Pain-tastique!" He punched the air with his fist. "Spore-free certainty."

There was a smattering of applause, mainly from the

Municipal Department men. "That's it, everybody," called the woman with the clipboard. And then to Nell and the two women, "Come this way."

She led them to a side room to meet with the mayor.

"Come to your senses, have you?" Nell's skin prickled under his gaze. The bag felt as though it was dragging around her waist. But he can't see it, she reminded herself. Xav had insisted the sweatshirt was big enough to conceal its bulk.

"My parents have what you want," she said. "But first you've got to agree to drop the warrant for Pear's arrest. And tell me where she is."

"Ah, here we go," said the mayor, just as Nell had expected. "I'll tell you when I've got what your parents stole—and not a moment before." He regarded her dispassionately, his raisin eyes giving nothing away. "Why the change of heart?"

"Perrine," she said. That, at least, was the truth.

"Where to, then? The sooner we head off, the sooner you'll get what you want."

"Gare du Nord," she said. "Ten o'clock. But when we get there, you have to let me go first. If they see you . . ." The chain of the bag was digging into her stomach. The rough crocodile skin was making her itch.

The mayor's face turned puce. Nell watched his sausage fingers curl into fists. His ring flashed. She imagined the blow, wondering how hard it would be, catching her on the cheek, and the pain that would follow. But it didn't come. Slowly, his fingers uncurled, and then—

"Grab her," he yelled suddenly to the Municipal Department men. "Hold her here until we get back."

"No!" shouted Nell. But it was too late. The mayor's order had taken her by surprise. The gray uniforms were surrounding her just as they had at the theater, and she didn't dare struggle in case they detected the bump of the bag. "You've got to take me with you!" she screamed. But no one was listening. The mayor, Cigarette Holder, and Lorgnette were already gone. The Municipal Department men moved back, shoving her for good measure, so that she stumbled and fell. The marble floor felt cold against her face. A tear slid down her cheek. She had been taken for a fool.

ell pummeled the floor with her hands. Screamed again. It was a scream of utter frustration. How *could* she have been so stupid? She shouldn't have told the mayor where they were going until she was in the car! *Then* he wouldn't have been able to get rid of her so easily.

Now he would turn up at Gare du Nord and, yes, he would find Melinda and Gerald, but there would be no bag and no incriminating gobbledygook. Nell felt like knocking her head against the wall. She couldn't allow the scoop to fail. She wouldn't!

Scrambling to her feet, she tugged at the door. Locked. She stood on a chair, but the window was too high. Her eyes roved wildly around the room. And there it was, a grate, or an air vent, she wasn't sure which, above the baseboard. With all her might, she wrenched it, once, twice, and miraculously it came away, clattering to the floor. Had anyone heard? She sat with her back to the hole just in case, waiting for a minute, breathing hard. No one came. She turned back to examine it. It was a small hole. But *she* was small.

Quickly, she slithered through. Dropped down. Grasped the flashlight in her pocket. Flicked it on. At this very moment, the mayor would be getting into his car. The doors would slam shut. The engine would rev. Nell squeezed her eyes tight shut. Conjured up those maps she had studied so long and so hard—Rue de Rivoli, Boulevard de Sébastopol, Boulevard de Strasbourg, Boulevard de Magenta, Rue de Dunkerque. If the traffic was light, they'd be at Gare du Nord in twenty minutes.

But . . . Nell allowed herself a sliver of hope. She was underground. And underground meant she must be near the Métro. In her head, she flipped the map over, her favorite map, the one where the creases were almost worn away to holes. Again she squeezed her eyes tight shut, conjured up the plan of the Métro. If she could get to Châtelet and jump on Line Four, there was the tiniest chance she might arrive there before them.

It was important to get her bearings. Not lose any time. They had parked in front of City Hall. They had walked in a straight line across the forecourt, up some steps, into the hall, and then into the side room. Surely she just had to retrace her steps, but underground this time, back the way she had come.

There was nothing else to do but follow her instincts, and her instincts said turn left, so she did, half running, half walking as best as she could by the light of the flashlight. And there they were. Ladder-type steps clinging to the wall. Up, up she climbed—and at the top, a manhole. She pushed against it with all her might, and as the light crashed in, she clambered out, pushing her hair out of her eyes and avoiding the surprised glances of the passersby on the street. She was on the Rue de Rivoli!

And then she ran like she had never run before, with the wind in her sails, dodging the shoppers, head down, elbows out, feet pounding along the sidewalk as though her life depended on it. She ran down the Rue de Rivoli until she reached the elegant green curve of the Métro entrance, and then she was careening down the steps and onto the platform, and joy of joys, a train was just rumbling in. Seven stops: Les Halles, Étienne Marcel, Réaumur-Sébastopol, Strasbourg–Saint-Denis, Château d'Eau, Gare de l'Est, Gare du Nord. *Come on, come on!* Why was it so slow? And then at last, off the train she leaped, along the platform, taking the steps two at a time, onto the concourse of Gare du Nord.

Now that she'd done it, now that she was here, she felt sick with nerves. She couldn't think! Her mind wouldn't stand still.

Get a grip, Nell, she said to herself.

She stood on tiptoe, straining to see through the crowds. The place was teeming. Announcements of departures and arrivals crackled over the loudspeakers; whistles blew, flags waved. Was she too late? Were they here? Had there already been a confrontation?

She was almost frantic with fear.

Reaching under her sweatshirt, she felt for the handbag, pulling the chain down over her hips and wriggling out of it. Tucking it under one arm, she flicked her eyes left, right, and center. It was imperative she saw them before they saw her.

And then, as if she had conjured them up just by *thinking* about them, there they were: the mayor, Cigarette Holder, and Lorgnette emerging from the crowds to her left. They were walking straight toward her, but they hadn't seen her yet. She had made it in time! She darted behind a pillar.

Now she could see Melinda and Gerald, still in fur hats and sunglasses, standing by the entrance to Platform Two. Nell looked back at the mayor. Even from here, she could see his tiny raisin eyes widen. He had seen the Magnificents.

She whipped her head back in the direction of her parents. For a split second, everything seemed to freeze. Was everyone here? Had Xav and company been able to rally everyone? And then: yes! She sensed the crowd growing, surging toward them, and in one great burst, she leaped out from behind the pillar and started to run across the concourse so fast she thought she might trip over her legs and fly through the air.

"Mummy," she panted, skidding to a halt in front of Melinda and thrusting the bag toward her as though it were a poisoned chalice.

"At last!" started Melinda impatiently.

A vein throbbed below Nell's eye. She only had a few seconds. "Mummy, we had a pact. You said you'd tell me about Pear if I got the bag—"

"Oh, do shut up," said Melinda. "This is neither the time nor the place."

"But you SAID!" shouted Nell, feeling the fury rise. The

mayor would be here in a minute, and all hell would break loose. "We made a deal!"

But Melinda had stopped listening, her expression turning from irritation to horror as the mayor appeared, swearing under his breath and trying to grab the bag in her hands.

"Get off! Gerald! Get him off me!"

"We had a deal," the mayor said, seething. He was so busy trying to snatch the bag from Melinda he had not yet seen Nell. "The spore is not free. You thought you could swipe it at our lunch and get away with it. Where's the one hundred thousand you agreed to pay me, eh?"

Melinda scowled. She wrenched the bag back. "We'll pay you when we see if it works," she spat. And then an ugly tug of war began that quickly became a battle as Gerald, Cigarette Holder, and Lorgnette joined in.

Nell blinked. Everyone was shouting, but she could only hear a kind of roaring in her ears. She blinked again. The station shifted, faded, and then . . . a burst of a flash, a click of a shutter. And more flashes and thousands more clicks, and suddenly Nell was back in the here and now and everything was loud and bright and the bag was dropped like a hot potato and the mayor's hand flew up to protect his face from the glare of the cameras and Melinda's eyes, black with anger, sought out Nell's.

But it didn't matter. The plan was working. Everyone had come. An enormous circle surrounded Nell and the mayor, Melinda and Gerald, Cigarette Holder and Lorgnette. There was no way out. It was a human fortress: masses and masses of children and grown-ups all brandishing baguettes and shouting angrily. A woman at the front—it was the lady from the haberdashery in Belleville—reached into a Pain-tastique bag and started to hurl croissants at the mayor.

She could see Michel but not Xav. Where was he? All the other familiar faces were here: the Bernards, the twins, Soutine and his family, Emil, and here came the police led by Neige, marching across the concourse.

Nell picked up the bag, retrieved the gobbledygook, and held it triumphantly aloft. *Now* the mayor saw her. His face turned scarlet. His eyes screwed themselves up into tiny burning balls of venom.

He didn't scare her.

"The mayor of Paris is elected to protect his citizens, not destroy them!" she cried. "But it is he who is behind the deadly spores that have been infecting the boulangeries of your city. We have proof that this man, Victor Henri, has

been closing your stores and opening his own ones—Pain-tastique—in their place. Quite simply, he has destroyed the livelihoods of innocent Parisians for his financial gain. And these two"—she pointed at Melinda and Gerald—"are planning something similar on their own shores."

Colette had elbowed her way to the front of the crowd. And now she linked arms with Nell. "It is all true!" she called out. And she didn't sound timid or unsure anymore. Her voice rang out clear and strong. "You can read the full story in *Le Monde* tomorrow!"

The crowd roared. And then a chant of "Liars! Cheats! Liars!" went up. "Liars! Cheats! Liars!" And linking arms, they advanced.

A scowl. A coyote-like wail, and then Cigarette Holder and Lorgnette were on either side of the mayor and were tearing straight for the human chain using their arms as batons. But it was no good—the people were furious, and they pushed them back, straight into the arms of the police.

"Penelope Magnificent, have you done this?" Melinda screeched as the police moved in and started to handcuff her. She looked deranged, her fur hat at half-mast and her sunglasses dangling from one ear. "Gerald, say something!"

But Gerald just stood with his mouth hanging open, his salesman's bravado all gone.

"Wait!" A high, clear voice.

It was Neige, standing stock-still and staring at Melinda as though she had just seen a ghost.

"Why is she staring at me like that?" spat Melinda. "Ouch! Mind my watch, it's valuable."

"It was *that* woman," cried out Neige, her voice spiraling up in excitement and shock, "who accused Perrine Chaumet of stealing."

TWENTY-NINE

The crowd, silent now, held their breath. Nell looked from Neige to Melinda and back again. She didn't understand.

"*She* was the client at Crown Couture. The one who accused Pear of taking her precious brooch. I didn't realize she was your mother, Nell!"

A frosty hand gripped Nell's heart. She took a step toward Melinda. "Why would you do that?"

"Oh, for goodness' sake, what does it matter now?" said Melinda. "I wish you would just stop going on about Pear! Pear this, Pear that! I don't know why you care about her so much."

"I do care about her," shouted Nell. "I've never stopped

caring about her." Sobs were fighting their way up her chest, into her throat, making it hard to speak.

"Well, you shouldn't," snapped Melinda. "She kidnapped you, for goodness' sake. She is nothing but a common criminal."

Nell stared at Melinda. Melinda stared back. There was nothing, *nothing* kind in that gaze. It was stony. Devoid of even a flicker of warmth.

And then, just like that, it made sense.

On the day they had been separated, the day of the argument and the shouting, they must have been going to run away together. To escape to Paris. But Melinda had found out. Sent Pear away. Banished Nell to boarding school.

"It's not kidnapping if you're leaving of your own free will," Nell yelled.

But her mother didn't even flinch. "Oh, you silly, silly girl," she said witheringly.

"Melinda . . ." warned Gerald.

"Oh, shut up," Melinda snapped. "What does it matter now? The stipulations can go to hell in a handbasket for all I care. We're ruined, anyway."

"What are you talking about?" burst out Nell. What did the boring old stipulations imposed by the boring old

Magnificent board have to do with her mother making false accusations about Pear?

"Penelope, the kidnapping you are referring to was the *second* attempt. Now, listen carefully." Melinda's eyes glittered. "She—stole—you—when—you—were—a—baby."

"What?"

"She stole you. How do you like that? I told you she was a criminal."

Nell felt like the earth had dropped away from beneath her. Is that why there was a warrant out for Pear's arrest? She opened her mouth, but no words came out. Pear had stolen her? From where?

"She made a mistake," continued Melinda. "A very big one. She'd be in jail if we hadn't come along and helped her out. And look at you now. I've never met anyone so ungrateful in my whole life."

"So . . ." The thought was enormous, like a volcano about to erupt. "You . . . you aren't my real parents, then?"

Melinda looked Nell up and down and smiled. A bitter, horrible, demonic smile. She shook the fur hat off, attempted to smooth her platinum-blond hair, difficult when handcuffed, but she managed it. "Well, no. I would have thought that was pretty obvious by now."

Nell felt as though she had been hit hard in the face.

Behind her, the crowd started to murmur. She could hear someone running across the concourse and shouting her name. "Nell! Nell!" The crowd parted. It was Xav, red-faced and panting, bent over now, trying to catch his breath.

"Nell! Don't listen to her. I went back to the theater and found out where Coco lives. She says to come."

The police agreed to let Nell go to Coco's as long as Michel accompanied her. There were questions to be asked, the inspector said, but they could wait. Somehow, they all managed to squeeze into a taxi by sitting on top of one another.

Everyone was chattering, reliving the scoop, congratulating themselves for the parts they had played. The plan had worked! The whole story would be splashed across the front page of *Le Monde* in the morning.

"You slept in the laundry cupboard?" Michel asked for the third time as the taxi racketed along the city streets, no less aghast than he had been when he heard it the first time around.

Nell nodded, squashed in the back seat with Soutine

and Neige on one side, Emil and Colette on the other, and Michel and Xav in the front, while Paul and Paulette crouched on the floor. Her mind was in a whirl. Melinda and Gerald weren't her real parents! Pear had kidnapped her when she was a baby. No wonder she was on the run. But if she was on the run, why would she have taken the time to finish the dress for Coco? And where was she now? The mayor had said she was out of the country. But who was to say he was telling the truth?

It was all so complicated. There was too much to take in. And she was scared. The person she had held steady in her mind all these years had started to go wobbly at the edges.

"Nell," Neige said, nudging her and looking at her questioningly. "You OK?"

She nodded, but she wasn't. She felt confused, bewildered. As if her inner compass—not the one that knew the streets of Paris, but the one that had always pointed her in the direction of Pear—was way off course.

"Give me the letter," said Neige, "the one in your pocket." Nell dug the letter out and handed it over.

"Darling Nell," read Neige.

"Everything was in place. I was going to come for you. But

something has happened and I need to set it right. Do not lose faith. We will be together and the truth will come out.

"*Your dearest friend, Pear.*

"*Do not lose faith,*" repeated Neige. "Nell, we're with you, we are your friends, and we're going to make sure you are all right."

THIRTY

When they rang the bell to Coco's apartment, Coco answered immediately. Seeing who her visitors were, her face broke out into a delighted grin, a million miles from the suspicion with which she had greeted Nell and Neige at the theater.

"I saw it on the news!" she cried, ushering them into a large living room. "You should all be feted. That was a marvelous thing you did. I always knew that mayor was bad news."

It was a beautiful apartment, with high ceilings and four large windows looking out onto the swaying treetops of the Boulevard Saint-Germain. One wall was lined with books—poetry and plays and stories—that Nell could see Neige's eyes were instantly drawn to; another wall was covered in paintings, giant canvases that seemed to hum and vibrate with splashy color. On the floor, a Turkish rug gleamed with reds and pinks and oranges, and there were two egg-shaped swivel chairs that the twins threw themselves into, imploring Xav and Soutine to spin them around. Colette and Emil stood side by side shyly, looking around the place with unconcealed awe.

Without the white gunk, Coco had the most expressive face Nell had ever seen. She was all eyes and nose and mouth, none of which seemed to fit, and yet altogether, her facial features were perfect. *"Chérie,"* she said, draping her arm around Nell's shoulders, leading her to a couch. "The fact that the Magnificents are embroiled in this spore thing will be music to Perri's ears. At last, she will be free!"

"Have you seen Pear, then? Where is she?" broke in Nell. There was so much to ask.

"Listen. I will explain everything," said Coco, plumping up the cushions of the couch and pushing Nell gently down. "But first let me get you all something to eat and drink. Emil, is it? Can you help me?"

Michel dusted down his coveralls and then lowered himself onto the sofa next to Nell. "The suspense, eh?" he said, his eyes twinkling. "I wish you and young Xavier had told me what was going on."

"Xav said not to," said Nell.

"He would say that. Thinks he can manage everything, but sometimes . . ."

"He managed really well," said Nell loyally. She looked over at Xav, who, with Soutine, was still spinning the twins around. He had gone to find Coco this morning. She hadn't asked him to, but he had known how much it meant to her.

"Here we are," said Coco, bearing a tray laden with glasses of lemonade. Emil followed, a plate in each hand piled high with sugary apple doughnuts. "They're not from Pain-tastique," said Coco quickly. "The boulangerie around the corner miraculously escaped the Thing."

When they had all collected a drink and a doughnut, and Coco had told them she didn't mind sugary fingerprints on the furniture—"It's nothing soap and warm water can't fix," she said—she made them all sit down. Xav squeezed in between Michel and Nell and gave her a reassuring smile.

"Perrine and I met when we were only fourteen," Coco began, sitting cross-legged in the middle of the rug so she had a clear view of everyone. "We were both runaways, and for a short while, we lived together in the tunnels because we had nowhere else to go."

"You lived in the tunnels?" exclaimed Michel. "At that age!"

"We did. And it wasn't only us two," said Coco, fixing her gaze on Nell. "Perri had a baby with her. And I think you know, Nell, that baby was you."

A collective gasp flashed around the room. There was a thud as Paul fell out of the egg-shaped chair. Neige, who had been reaching for a book, stopped still, one arm frozen in midair.

"So she *did* steal me," said Nell. Why would Pear do that? "Who from?"

"Stop it! She didn't steal you," said Coco fiercely, rising onto her knees. "She saved you. She didn't want you to suffer the same fate that she had."

"What fate?" Nell had an image of Pear as Rapunzel again, her face pressed up against a narrow window, calling to be let out.

"Fourteen years of heartlessness. Of loneliness. Of being told she was worth nothing and would never amount to anything," said Coco with great feeling.

It sounded strangely familiar, thought Nell. In her head, she could hear Melinda and Gerald calling her a tiresome sneak, over and over again.

"She grew up in a children's home run by an awful couple called Monsieur and Madame Besset. She was a foundling. Do you know what that is?"

"An abandoned baby," offered Paul. He was back in the egg-shaped chair, but both he and Paulette had stopped spinning. Pear had always been telling stories about foundlings and runaways, and Nell was starting to understand why.

"That's right, Paul. Foundlings never know who their real mothers and fathers are." For a split second, a cloud passed across Coco's face, and then Nell remembered the headline splashed across *Paris Match* below Coco's picture. "From Rags to Riches: Parisian Foundling Makes it Big!" She felt a tug of sympathy for Coco. Coco was a foundling, too, and she would have her own story to tell.

"When she turned thirteen," continued Coco, "the Bessets sent Perri out to learn needlework at the house of a lady nearby. It opened Perri's eyes; she glimpsed another world. She adored the craft and found she had an aptitude for it. But then the woman moved away, the visits stopped, and life went horribly back to normal."

As the story slumped, Coco sprang up. She had the grace of a cat, a lightness of movement, thought Nell. She began to prowl back and forth across the rug.

"She couldn't bear it any longer!" burst out Coco, making them all jump. "So she decided to run away. The time was right. She was fourteen. Old enough to get an apprenticeship."

"Just like you, Neige," said Paulette.

"But on the morning she left, as she crept through the sleeping house, she heard a tiny mewling sound coming from the kitchen."

"Was it . . . ?" asked Xav.

"She thought it might be a kitten, so she went to look. But it was not a kitten. It was a baby, tucked up in the dresser drawer, far away from the Bessets' room so they could sleep undisturbed."

Coco paused. It was very odd, thought Nell. Coco still *looked* like Coco, and yet she had *become* Pear. They all watched, mesmerized as Coco-Pear gazed down at the imaginary drawer, torn between not knowing whether to stay or run away. Nell could see why she was such a celebrated actor. Gently, Coco picked up the little bundle. Cradled it in her arms. Nell felt tears pricking her eyes.

"It was déjà vu!" said Coco. "Perri herself had been in that very same drawer fourteen years before. Perhaps she should have just walked right by. But how could she turn away from such a tiny, innocent, defenseless baby?"

"Of course she couldn't!" burst out Xav.

"*I* would have taken you," said Neige, turning to Nell with shiny eyes.

"And me," said the twins together. And Nell could tell

from the look on Soutine's face that he would have taken her, too.

"The short story is, she *did* take you. And in Paris, after we met, we took turns looking after you while she went out seeking apprenticeships and I auditioned. It was 1957. We lived in a lovely cavern—we made it so homely. We called you P'tit Minou because your cries sounded like a tiny kitten's."

The fruit-box cradle! The one Mimi had tucked her little mouse-flashlight in. *That* had Minou scratched on it. It must have been Nell's!

"But then you got sick. And it got to be too much, and . . . Perri saw the advertisement on the bulletin board at the American Church."

Coco stopped. Her expression was grave. "Remember, she was young. We had no money. What else could she do?"

"What was this advertisement?" asked Michel, frowning.

"From a couple desperate to adopt a baby."

"Melinda and Gerald," said Nell slowly. "But I don't understand. How *could* they be desperate? If they were desperate, they would have loved me, wouldn't they? They never cared for me one iota!"

"It was something to do with the Magnificent board and the sti—stip—" Coco grasped for the words and then stopped, eyes wide. Outside, footsteps could be heard thundering up the stairs. The door flew open.

"The stipulations!"

Nell's mouth dropped open. Standing in the doorway was a young woman, face flushed, golden curls caught up in a green velvet ribbon.

The woman stepped inside. "It was all to do with the hateful stipulations," she cried.

Another gasp ricocheted around the room. The timing couldn't have been more perfect. This was better than any live theater show.

"Pear?" Nell rubbed her eyes. Rubbed them again.

"Nell!" cried Pear.

A warmth like Nell had never felt before flooded her entire being. The thing she had hoped and waited for and dreamed of for all these years was finally coming true!

Pear was here! And she was striding across the room toward her. And everyone was cheering and whooping, and Nell was certain she saw Xav brushing away a tear.

"I came as quickly as I could," said Pear, grasping Nell's hands in her own. Nell felt her chest rise and swell and then crash in a wave of sheer happiness.

Pear was here! She had come! She had kept her word.

Nell had always known, deep down, she could trust Pear.

Nell threw herself into Pear's arms and then she was sobbing and Pear was sobbing, and Paul and Paulette were doing a sort of mad polka around the room, and then Coco was flinging herself on them, too—"Reunited, a family again!"—and Xav and Neige and the others were grinning from ear to ear, and there was laughter and tears and Nell felt delirious with happiness.

She and Pear had been apart for so long, and yet everything felt right, and nothing, nothing had changed.

———

It was all the fault of the stipulations, explained Pear. Melinda and Gerald could only inherit Magnificent Foods if they were able to prove that they had an heir. "It's called the Magnificent clause," she said. "There was a distant cousin in America who already had a child. They were worried that if they didn't act quickly, the company would go to him."

It was dawn, and Nell and Pear were sitting on the Quai d'Orsay, a short stroll from Coco's apartment. Their legs dangled over the Seine, the water rippling like silvery feathers in the early morning breeze. They hadn't slept. They had too much to talk about. But Nell didn't feel the slightest bit tired.

"Oh, Nell, I thought I had found us both a home . . . and some security. It seemed so perfect. They wanted me to come and take care of you, and of course I came because I couldn't bear to be parted from you. But as soon as we got to London, I understood why they wanted you and saw that I had made a terrible mistake."

"But *we* were happy, you and me," said Nell.

"We were," said Pear. "I was determined to give you all the love that they couldn't, and for a while that worked, especially since most of the time they stayed out of our way. But then I discovered that they were going to ship you off to boarding school and send me back to Paris. Melinda had even arranged the apprenticeship for me at Crown Couture. A sort of bribe, I suppose, and so I determined that we would run away."

"How could I have forgotten that? It didn't come clear in my memory until today," said Nell.

"You were so young," said Pear, squeezing Nell's arm. "I'm not sure you really understood what was happening. Anyway, they caught us just as we were leaving. Said I couldn't have it both ways. There was a terrible scene. Melinda threatened to call the police and get me arrested for kidnapping you in the first place. And, oh . . . I don't know." Pear wiped her eyes and sighed. "She was the more powerful one with all the money and the connections."

"So you went . . ." said Nell.

"Yes. But I vowed that as soon as I had made something of myself, and as soon as I could support you, I would come back and get you."

"And you nearly did."

"Six months ago, I wrote to Melinda telling her I was going to go to the police and come clean. I was going to admit to taking you from the children's home. I wanted to do it properly this time—no more sneaking away in the middle of the night."

"But she didn't like that . . ." said Nell.

"She didn't like it at all. Instead, she planted her brooch on me at Crown Couture and made me out to be a thief. I lost my job. I couldn't pay the rent on my apartment. I was in danger of becoming destitute all over again. Thank goodness for Coco. It was pure coincidence when she ordered a dress from Crown Couture and we became friends again. When I lost my job, she asked me to finish the dress for her privately and suggested I move in."

"That's when you wrote me this," said Nell, drawing the letter out of her pocket. "But where does the mayor fit in? Why did *he* issue a warrant for your arrest?"

"Because being dismissed from Crown Couture didn't stop me," Pear said fiercely. "I wouldn't give up. I wrote to the Magnificent board, laying everything bare. When

Melinda and Gerald found out, they must've been furious. It was they who asked the mayor to issue a warrant for my arrest. I imagine it was initially part of the deal they were striking over this Spore Thirteen."

"But Melinda and Gerald were too greedy," said Nell.

"Yes, Nell! They stole the recipe for this . . . Thing, instead of honoring their agreement. And then the mayor, desperate to get it back, saw an opportunity to blackmail YOU into helping him."

She paused to hug Nell again. "But you were too clever."

"And *were* you out of the country?" asked Nell. "The whole time I've been here?"

"I must have been on my way to London when you were on your way here," said Pear. "I went with Coco's lawyer to meet with the Magnificent board and a representative from Scotland Yard."

"But are you going to be OK?" said Nell as a new wave of worry washed over her. "Is there still a warrant out for your arrest?"

"I'm seeing the inspector tomorrow," said Pear, "with the lawyer and the chap from Scotland Yard. They think it will be OK. They say I have a good case."

"We did it together," said Nell.

"We did," said Pear. "Oh, Nell, you don't know how often

I've worried that I did the wrong thing all those years ago. Perhaps if I had left you with the Bessets, one day your *real* mother might have come back to claim you."

Nell was quiet for a moment. It was true that she would never know who her real mother and father were—or find out whether she had been wanted or not. But Pear had found her. Pear had fought for her. She had not abandoned her.

"Pear, you wanted me," she said. "And I want you. And that's enough."

EPILOGUE

Every day now, Nell woke with a smile. How could she *not* smile when the first thing she saw was blue sky and Parisian rooftops outside her tiny casement window, when she knew that Pear was alive and well and working to clear her name, when for the first time in years, her life stretched out in front of her unimpeded by trouble and full of possibility and promise.

Very quickly, Nell's days took on a pattern. In the mornings, she would swing out of bed and pull on her brand-new scarlet uniform. The pants were the right length, and she no longer had to breathe in to button them; she didn't have to hide her hair under her cap, either.

After the whole story had been splashed across *Le Monde*, Monsieur Jacques had wasted no time in declaring

Nell an official bell girl. He had marched straight into the director's office and demanded it. All the hotel staff had cheered like crazy when the announcement was made.

"I suppose it'll keep you out of trouble," Michel had said, eyes twinkling, and Nell and Xav had both jumped around in glee. She was good at it. She enjoyed it. And there were still two weeks to go before school started. French school. For the moment, Nell was staying with Michel and Xav in their attic rooms. The twins' mother, who worked in City Hall's Child Protection Department, had organized it. It was the perfect solution, everyone agreed, even though a tiny part of Nell missed the coziness of her bed in the laundry room.

Soon, once everything was settled, Nell would be going to live with Pear and Coco in the apartment on the Boulevard Saint-Germain. In the meantime, she saw them every day, usually at lunchtime, in the Tuileries or the Jardin du Luxembourg, where they would laze on the grass and eat bread and apples and cheese. It was a precious time that they all treasured, before Coco's matinees and in between Pear's meetings with the police and her lawyers.

After lunch, Nell would meet up with Xav and Paul and Paulette, and they'd sprint through the tunnels to Chez Ben Amor, where they were helping Soutine and his family redecorate the shop in time for the grand reopening planned for the following week.

Now that the spore had been identified, scientists had invented an antidote, and slowly all the boulangeries were getting back on their feet. The Bernards, too, had moved out of the cave and back into their premises on the Rue Mouffetard. And Mimi was determined to tempt Nell back down to the catacombs.

Sometimes Nell would catch the Métro to Belleville and meet up with Emil for a lemonade. He had taught her how to swing backward on the bars, and she could dangle upside down now for hours. He was still caring for Pear's cat, Sylvie, because Coco's landlord wouldn't allow any pets. Colette, he told Nell with pride in his eyes, had been promoted from editor's secretary to junior reporter.

Most days at six, Nell would meet Neige outside Crown Couture, always bringing along a pile of Coco's books for Neige to read. She devoured them, tearing through the pages and then discussing them with Coco afterward. Meanwhile, Aunt Sophie grew stronger by the day. At Christmastime, she would return to work, and Neige would be able to leave Crown Couture and go back to school. Her ambition, she told Nell, was to study philosophy at the Sorbonne.

It was on one of these days when Nell was lurking around on the Rue du Faubourg Saint-Honoré—out of sight in case Madame Josette or Valérie spotted her—that the door opened and Monsieur Crown burst out. Terrified, Nell shrank back. She really didn't want a repeat performance of their first encounter.

"Come, come," he said, as though an angry word had never been spoken between them. "Wait until you see—"

"But . . ." Nell looked down to check if she was wearing what she thought she was wearing. She was. How odd. He didn't appear to be withering at the sight of her sweatshirt and jeans.

Monsieur Crown was already dashing back in, his round pin-striped form bobbing along ahead of her, so she pushed through the door and followed him up the narrow winding stairs.

"Voilà!" he said, bouncing aside so that Nell came face-to-face with a dress the likes of which had never been seen before in Paris. It was an extravagant gown made entirely from a patchwork of red sweatshirt and blue denim. "The Penelope dress," he said with a sweeping bow, "in honor of you, Mademoiselle, who so courageously saved the city's boulangeries—and to say sorry for our role in the disappearance of Pear."

He looked so sheepish, and the dress so outlandish, that Nell burst out laughing. She had been named after a bag. And now a dress had been named after her!

"It's lovely, Monsieur." It was the unexpectedness of it that delighted her. She held the dress up against her and spun around. The denim parts whipped and the sweatshirt pieces swirled and she went around and around until the world went dizzy, and when she stopped, she had to grasp Monsieur Crown's arm to steady herself. "There's just one thing," she said. "Can we call it the Nell dress? *That* is my name."

Paris Match

DECEMBER, 1969

On Saturday, the actor Mademoiselle Coco Swann and the couturier Mademoiselle Perrine Chaumet hosted a reception at the Hotel de Crillon for all the bakers of Paris and their children. It has been six months since the ex-mayor, Victor Henri, was arrested and charged with sabotaging hundreds of boulangeries in order to expand his own empire. Investigative reporter

Colette Colbert has since uncovered vast under-ground cellars stockpiled with wine—intended to be distributed under the label Vin-tastique—once existing supplies had been contaminated with Spore Thirteen.

The occasion at the Crillon also celebrated the launch of Atelier Pear, the new label set up by Chaumet with financial backing from Swann. During the toast, Mademoiselle Chaumet made the surprise announcement that she has been granted permission by the French and British authorities to officially adopt a twelve-year-old child named Penelope Magnificent, henceforth known as Nell Minou Chaumet-Swann. It was a glittering occasion, with excellent canapés provided by the Ben Amors of the Rue des Martyrs.

ACKNOWLEDGMENTS

The Pear Affair emerged from a patchwork of ideas, but it would never have been written without Paris. I've loved the city ever since my first visit with my family age twelve (yes! we ventured down into the catacombs!) and then with my French host Fabienne, who introduced me to so many very French things: the department stores on Boulevard Haussmann, slabs of chocolate sandwiched between crusty bread, and her mum's delicious Potage Bonne Femme.

Paris was also where my boyfriend and I went on our first vacation together, halfway through our Art Foundation course. It was winter, and we spent hours at the Pompidou Center, him listening to music in the library, me in the bookshop. We wore not-warm-enough suede jackets, huddled on benches in the Tuileries eating baguettes and cheese, and lurked around in the Louvre. That very same boyfriend is now my husband!

As a fashion student, I made a beeline for Paris twice a year to sneak into the catwalk shows. I was quite good at nipping past the guards when they were looking the other way! In between shows, I trawled the haberdashery stores in Montmartre, ate dessert at Galeries Lafayette, dinner at Chartier, and discovered my all-time favorite flea market in the tiny Place d'Aligre. The all-you-can-eat dessert buffet is long gone, and Chartier is now on the tourist trail, but the flea market is still there and still wonderful.

Writing a book is very much a collaborative matter. So thanks to my writers group: Tim, Lis, Graham, and especially Heather—for spurring me on with your perceptive, thoughtful advice. Thank you to Tessa David, my agent, for championing me and always being so encouraging. And to the wiz that is Alice Swan: you are the most fabulous editor. Thank you so much for trusting me to get on with it and then just knowing how to get me to make it better, every time.

Special thanks to my US editor, the brilliant Susan Van Metre—so happy to be in your orbit! To designer Maya

Tatsukawa for making *The Pear Affair* look so good; and to the rest of the team at Walker Books US. Thank you Jo Rioux for your amazing illustrations. I adore them.

Last but not least, to my lovely family: Moira, Margot, and Lucy; Nick, Rose, and Poppy—*merci infiniment*, you are the best!

ABOUT THE AUTHOR & ILLUSTRATOR

JUDITH EAGLE'S career thus far has included stints as a stylist, fashion editor, and features writer. She now spends her mornings writing and her afternoons working in a secondary school library. *The Pear Affair* is her second novel. She lives with her family and her cat, Stockwell, in South London.

JO RIOUX is an author and illustrator who studied illustration at Sheridan College in Canada. She has illustrated young adult novels, chapter books, picture books, and graphic novels, including *Cat's Cradle: The Golden Twine*, which won a Joe Shuster Dragon Award for best comic for kids, and *The Daughters of Ys* by M. T. Anderson. She lives in Ottawa.